Henry H. M. Carnavon, George Sydenham Clarke

The Defence of the Empire

A Selection From the Letters and Speeches of Henry Howard Molyneux, Fourth Earl

of Carnarvon - Edited by Sir George Sydenham Clarke

Henry H. M. Carnavon, George Sydenham Clarke

The Defence of the Empire
A Selection From the Letters and Speeches of Henry Howard Molyneux, Fourth Earl of Carnarvon - Edited by Sir George Sydenham Clarke

ISBN/EAN: 9783337167974

Printed in Europe, USA, Canada, Australia, Japan

Cover: Foto ©Andreas Hilbeck / pixelio.de

More available books at **www.hansebooks.com**

THE

DEFENCE OF THE EMPIRE

A SELECTION FROM THE LETTERS AND SPEECHES OF

HENRY HOWARD MOLYNEUX,

FOURTH EARL OF CARNARVON.

EDITED BY

Lieut.-Col. Sir GEORGE SYDENHAM CLARKE
R.E., K.C.M.G., F.R.S.

WITH A MAP.

LONDON :

JOHN MURRAY, ALBEMARLE STREET.
1897.

PREFACE.

In 1878, when for a time war with Russia
appeared imminent, the shadow of a great
fear fell upon the Empire. The navy of
the Tsar was wholly unequal to a contest
with Great Britain, and in the Black Sea
had been completely neutralized by the fleet
created by Abd-ul-Aziz. It was quickly
realized, however, that all over the world
British ports filled with valuable shipping
lay open to the attack of any armed vessel
which might succeed in reaching them,
and that British towns containing a
wealth of national and private resources
were exposed to insult and injury. Strong
as was the fleet relatively to that of
Russia, this was a period of comparative
naval depression, which continued till

1889. French ship-building, checked by
the military disasters of 1870-71, had
shown a marked revival. The vote of six
millions, hurriedly obtained by the British
Government, was in part devoted to the
purchase of ships; but, in other respects,
the practical effect of this outlay could
not be felt for a considerable time. The
Empire, as a whole, was totally unprepared for the stress of a great war, and
perhaps for the first time Greater Britain
awoke to its needs. Some Colonies, on
their own initiative, at once made provision for local defence, and indifferent
armaments were hastily shipped from
England to be provisionally mounted for
the defence of the more important coaling
stations.

In 1859 a Royal Commission had been
appointed to consider the defences of the
naval ports of the United Kingdom, and
in 1861 a Select Committee had reported
upon Colonial Military Expenditure. It
is, however, correct to state that the whole

question of Imperial Defence had been absolutely ignored ; that no inquiry into the means by which commerce might be protected in war had ever been under- taken, and that no clear idea of the relative strategic importance of the many Imperial ports had been attained.

Enquiry was now demanded, and in 1879 a strong Royal Commission, presided over by the late Earl of Carnarvon, met to consider and report upon " the defence of British possessions and commerce abroad." The labours of the Commis- sion extended over nearly three years. A mass of important evidence was brought together ; invaluable statistics were com- piled ; the strategic posts and coaling stations of the Empire were authoritatively pointed out, and schemes of local defence were examined and presented.

The three voluminous Reports of the Commission have never been made public; but the short abridgment laid before the Colonial Conference in 1887, enables a fair estimate to be formed of the scope and thoroughness of this momentous investigation.

The First Report, dated 3rd September, 1881, deals with the Cape of Good Hope, the maintenance of troops in British Honduras, armaments, shipping and trade routes. The vital importance of the Cape, half-forgotten since the opening of the Suez Canal, was forcibly recalled. It was pointed out that " circumstances may arise, when the sea route through the Mediterranean will be attended with such risks that it may have to be abandoned by ships not prepared to defend themselves." It was estimated that in such circumstances, cargoes of the annual value of £200,000,000 sterling would move *via* the Cape. The immense and growing preponderance of British tonnage was shown, and the gradual supersession of sailing ships by steamers was brought to light. Thirteen great imperial trade routes of the world were distinguished.

In the Second Report, the duties of the Navy and its tremendous responsibilities in war were admirably defined. The vital question of the Navy had not been referred to the Commissioners; but, overstepping the limits of their charter, they called attention, in significant words, to the weakness of the right arm of the Empire: "We are deeply impressed by the Returns furnished by the Admiralty, and to these, as well as to the other evidence, we invite the particular attention of your Majesty's Government, feeling bound to express our opinion that looking to the action of other countries, the strength of the Navy should be increased with as little delay as possible." The rest of this volume is devoted to a careful examination of the defensive requirements and resources of the Australasian colonies.

The final Report, dated 22nd July, 1882, dealt with the defence of the great trade routes previously defined. Coaling stations were selected and their defences discussed.

It is justly stated that "not until the important coaling stations shall have been made secure can the strength of the British Navy be adequately exerted at sea. When, however, this has been accomplished, no other Power will possess equal facilities for keeping fleets at sea, or equally good lines of communications."

To the work of the Commission, Lord Carnarvon brought all his earnestness of purpose. It was to him no mere temporary duty to be discharged and then forgotten, but a task of Imperial importance, the accomplishment of which involved the greatest of national interests. As early as 1862, he had, in the House of Lords drawn attention to the whole question of Colonial Defence, pointing out the necessity for a scientific classification of fortified ports, deprecating expenditure upon the Ionian Islands, and pleading for the application of intelligible principles to the policy of Imperial fortifications. " I desire," he stated, "to see our Colonial expenditure on fortifications regulated on some definite principle. At present there seems to be no principle at all. While in some places, we economize unwisely, we lavish our money on other places where there could be no advantage proportionate to the outlay." In this remarkable speech, many of the recommendations of the Royal Commission are plainly foreshadowed, and other problems, still unsolved, are indicated. "There is," said Lord Carnarvon, "no more pressing question than the relationship between the Mother Country and the Colonies in regard to military expenditure. It is not a mere matter of money—interest, honour, sentiment and humanity are alike involved . . . duties and rights go hand in hand, and the people who are desirous of enjoying the privileges of constitutional freedom must be prepared to make some sacrifices in return for that inestimable boon." This last sentence goes to the very root of the great question of Imperial Defence.

Thus, sixteen years before the appointment of the Commission, Lord Carnarvon showed how thoroughly he had grasped the growing needs of the Empire.

The Report bears the impress of the knowledge and the anxious care which he devoted to its preparation. At length great principles were formulated, and the mutual obligations of the Mother Country and the Colonies were defined. At length a clear light was thrown alike upon the defensive needs of the Empire and the means of satisfying them. Henceforth, vagueness of thought and purposeless expenditure could admit of no justification. Definite aims and distinct objects were set before Her Majesty's Government, and reasoning replaced the "hypothetical suggestions" of which Sheridan, nearly a century before, had rightly complained.

It may justly be stated that the Commission marked a new departure in the national history.

The great trust which Lord Carnarvon had gladly accepted did not end with the presentation of the final Report. A further duty—voluntarily entered upon—was still to be undertaken. Enquiries of this nature, dealing with subjects however grave, too frequently pass into swift oblivion. Frequently commenced with a view to silence a temporary agitation, or to supply a plea for inaction, they serve their purpose, and are relegated to convenient obscurity. Our political annals team with such instances. It is the exception rather than the rule for the recommendations of Royal Commissions to be translated into action, and their chairmen and members often appear to readily acquiesce in the extinction of the schemes they have proposed.

This easy abnegation of a great responsibility was impossible to Lord Carnarvon. When nearly a year had passed without any steps being taken to protect the Imperial harbours, and to guard the trade routes on which the very life of the nation depends, he began to earnestly address himself to his further task. How persistently, throughout a period of six years, he strove to warn the country of its dangers, and how urgently he pleaded for the measures which the Commission had formulated, this little volume abundantly shows. In speech and in writing, in London and in Australia, with unflagging energy in spite of profound discouragement, he continued to labour for the cause he had at heart.

The labour was not in vain. Much for which Lord Carnarvon strenuously pleaded has been accomplished. All the coaling stations selected by the Commission are now sufficiently fortified. The strategic points of King George's Sound and Thursday Island have been protected by the patriotic efforts of the Australasian Colonies. Table Bay and Simon's Bay have substantial defences, and the Government of the Colony has in consideration important measures for increasing its military force. Canada, the inadequacy of whose militia was pointed out by Lord Carnarvon in 1862, has since made marked progress, and has recently rearmed her troops with the service rifle and the latest field gun. Esquimalt has been at length dealt with by the War Office in co-operation with the Dominion. From Plymouth through the Mediterranean to Hong Kong, or by the Cape route and Mauritius to Ceylon and the Bay of Bengal, protected coaling stations stand ready for the service of the fleet. The great harbours of Australasia are all provided with defences. Crown Colonies, such as Mauritius, Ceylon, the Straits, and Hong Kong have shared in the necessary expenditure. Others have shown willingness to make sacrifices in order to guard their integrity. Meanwhile, the establishment of the excellent Military College at Kingston, Canada, accomplished under Lord Carnarvon's directions, has borne rich fruit. This

institution, to the inauguration of which
he looked back with "the greatest satisfaction," has not only raised the standard
of military acquirements in the Dominion,
but has supplied valuable officers to the
British Army.

The national armour is not yet complete
at all points.   More remains to be done.
As Lord Carnarvon pointed out, "the
question of garrisons cannot be separated
from the question of fortifications." Measures for strengthening the garrisons of
some coaling stations are now under consideration.   In every part of the Empire,
progress has been made.   "I have few
practical objects in politics more near to
my heart," said Lord Carnarvon at Melbourne in 1887, "than to see the great
stations abroad where the Queen's Navy
must be refitted, where it must be coaled,
where it must receive from time to time
protection, placed in a position of complete and adequate defence."   This object
may almost be said to be attained, and

already the naked defencelessness of the Empire in 1878 is half-forgotten.

In the speeches and papers now republished will be found allusions to matters of Imperial politics with which defence is closely involved. The relations between the mother country and the Colonies occupied a great place in Lord Carnarvon's mind, as the Melbourne speech testifies. In memorable words, he sought to impress upon Australia the duty of "patience, support and forbearance" in the international questions which must frequently confront and perplex the Imperial Government. This lesson was not unneeded. Wisely he dwelt upon the bond of sympathy, which is perhaps more strongly felt in Great Britain than in the Colonies, and emphatically he asserted that "the sun of English enterprise and courage has not gone down."

The future depends wholly upon the united effort of the Empire. The national resources are unrivalled. To so organize

I.D.   *b*

them that they may be ready for a time of trial would be the greatest work which a patriot or statesman could accomplish. It is a work which cannot be hurried. Time and the spread of knowledge of the true principles of Imperial Defence are alike required. Looking back, however, it is impossible not to be struck with the progress already achieved. To the miserable weakness which prevailed in 1878 and later, has succeeded a measure of strength which we in common with Foreign Powers do not fully recognize.

The Royal Commission of 1878 was undoubtedly the starting-point of this great movement. To Lord Carnarvon belongs the honour of earnestly endeavouring to supply the sustained impulse, failing which little would have been accomplished. And when, in the future, historians come to examine the causes which led to the transformation of a condition of extreme national peril into one of comparative security his devoted services to the Empire will be gratefully acknowledged.

CONTENTS.

THE

DEFENCE OF THE EMPIRE.

I.

BRITISH POSSESSIONS ABROAD.

Speech in the House of Lords on 4th May, 1883.

THE EARL OF CARNARVON asked whether Her Majesty's Government could give any assurance that they were taking any measures with a view to carrying into effect at an early date the recommendations of the Royal Commission for the defence of British possessions and commerce abroad.

The Commission (he continued) of which I had the honour to be chairman, was appointed nearly four years ago, and consisted of Lord Camperdown, Sir Henry Holland, Sir Alexander

I.D.   B

1883. Milne, Sir Lintorn Simmons, Sir Henry
Barkly, Mr. Whitbread, Mr. Hamilton, Mr.
Childers, and Sir Thomas Brassey. We sat
for three years, and reported at very considerable length, as is known to the Government. We reported by instalments in order
to enable the Government to take action without delay upon those questions which we considered to be of the greatest and most urgent
importance. The report of the Commission
has not been laid upon the table of the House.
It is of a strictly confidential character, and I
should not be justified in bringing the recommendations before the House, nor in saying
anything to induce the Government to take
that course. But those recommendations, based
as they were to an extraordinary extent on professional evidence, are very important, and it
is with regret that I have not seen any action
taken by Her Majesty's Government on the
subject. I trust that I am mistaken in this,
and that the report has not been consigned

to the pigeon-hole. At any rate the time may come when it may be said to the members of the Commission, "Why did you, knowing the vast interests involved and what the recommendations were, sit absolutely silent and passive while you thought or saw no action was being taken?" I will not have that on my conscience, and after this I shall place the whole responsibility on the shoulders of the Government.

There are some things which I may say without indiscretion, because the facts to which I shall refer are already in a great measure public property. I will not read many figures to the House, but I will lay a few before it in order to show the enormous stake which the country had in this matter, although those figures hardly convey a full impression of it. In 1878, since which year there has, no doubt, been a considerable increase, the value of British shipping— ships alone — was estimated at £88,000,000,

1883. and that of colonial shipping at £20,000,000, a total of £108,000,000. To that must be added the annual value of the foreign trade of the United Kingdom, which amounted to the sum of £620,000,000 ; and of the colonial trade, exclusive of trade with the United Kingdom, £190,000,000, or a total of £810,000,000 sterling. Yet I have excluded many items which might have been fairly added to this large amount.

But, my lords, enormous as the figures are, they barely represent the entire value of the interests at stake. The value of the trade of the United Kingdom, and of the ships engaged in it afloat at one time, is close upon £150,000,000 sterling, and not only is there no other country or people in the world which has as large a stake as this, but it is a stake so large that, as I have said, the figures give really little idea of it. Further, I will compare the merchant navy of England with that of the rest of the world in 1880,

the latest figures I have. The total tonnage 1883
of the British merchant navy was 6,500,000
tons, of which the steam tonnage amounted
to no less than 2,700,000 tons. On the other
hand, the total foreign tonnage of ships of every
nation included amounted to only 8,000,000
tons, and their steam tonnage was considerably less than ours.

I will go one step further, and remind the
House of that which is no secret, that during
the last few years sailing ships have been to
an enormous extent superseded by steamers.
In 1860 the total of British tonnage engaged
in the home and foreign trade was 4,250,000
tons, and of that only 400,000 tons represented steam ; while in 1879 the total tonnage
of British ships in the home and foreign trade
had increased to 6,250,000 tons, of which
steamers represented no less than 2,300,000
tons. It is no exaggeration to say that a
complete revolution has been effected by the
supersession of sailing ships by steam. Many

1883. questions arise on this matter, into which I need not enter; but there is one point the vital importance of which no one will dispute who has looked into the subject—the defence of our coaling stations abroad. It is vitally necessary for this reason, that unless our coaling stations are in an effective state our fleets cannot operate against an enemy; we shall not be able to shelter our merchantmen, to repair and refit our ships, and, in short, we shall not be able to make use of the superior powers of steam which we possess as a nation. Your lordships will remember the amount of mischief that was done by a few ships, such as the *Alabama* and *Florida,* in the time of the American war. But, great as that mischief was, it would be nothing compared to that which might be done to our shipping in a time of war if these coaling stations are not properly cared for. We stand in a totally different position in this respect from any

other nation in the world. Trade supplies the 1883.
sinews of this country, and our trade, unlike
that of every other nation, is scattered over the
surface of the globe. France is the only other
country that has colonies and a considerable
amount of commerce, and I wish to point
out to your lordships that the French have
thought it expedient to take steps for the
defence of their coaling stations at Senegal,
Réunion, and other places. At Martinique
also they have spent considerable sums, and
are building a dry dock there capable of holding very large ships.

I will read to the House an extract from
a speech made by the French Minister of
Marine two or three years ago, when he
brought his estimates before the French
Chamber, and your lordships will see that
it is very applicable to the present question.
He said: " Our colonies ought to be rendered
safe from insult, by which I mean that a
single ship should not be able to place itself

1883 in front of one of the towns on the coast
and summon it to furnish either coal or
provisions on pain of bombardment. If there
were no works capable of resisting and
replying with guns to this sort of requisition
we should be obliged to submit, even though
we were masters at sea. It is said that ships
of war should supply the want, but they
could not be everywhere, and it is possible
that a hostile cruiser, taking advantage of
their temporary absence, might descend upon
an important port and levy contributions
which would far exceed in value the cost of
the defences we propose. In conclusion, it is
necessary for you to decide whether the
colonies are or are not to be defended, and
let me say that if you decide that they are
not to be defended you will probably lose far
more by the disasters which may ensue than
the cost of fortifications. I have done my duty
by laying the matter before you as I thought
was right, and thus relieved myself from the

responsibility which must have rested upon 1883.
me if by my silence I had been the cause of
an insult to the French flag. You wish to
keep the colonies. You are right, but in
order to hold them it is absolutely necessary
to arm them."

Those words may be applied to our own
case. If the French Minister thought it right
to speak in such terms, the question is certainly one which should engage the attention
of the Parliament of this country. There is
one other point to which I should like to
call the attention of the House. There is a
constant tendency out of doors to confuse
the colonies with mere military stations; but
the cases are distinct. I think the colonies
properly so called are doing their duty very
fairly in this matter. In Australia, at Sydney,
at Adelaide, and at Melbourne, very important
works are being constructed, and so keen are
the colonists in this matter that they have
adopted some of the latest changes in the

1883. construction of guns, and in addition many
of them have already created considerable
land forces. The self-governing colonies are
in fact in most cases commencing to do what
is necessary in the matter, and are doing it
without putting us to one shilling of expense.
The principle on which they are acting is
that if we with our squadron protect them,
they, on the other hand, will give shelter to
our ships by placing their ports in a state
of defence.

I now turn to the military stations, and
of them, of course, a principal part of the
expense falls, and must fall, on this country;
but at the same time, they are absolutely
essential, and if they are placed and kept
in a sufficient state of defence, there is every
reason to hope that in time of war we may
clear the sea of our enemies. I consider
that I ought to make no reference to the
specific recommendations of the Royal Commission; and this only I will say, that

some of those recommendations involved comparatively little cost, and further, that in any
recommendations we made we were most
careful to avoid recommending any multipli-
cation of garrisons or forces. I will only add
one word more in deprecation of the idea
that because we hold Egypt we are therefore able to dispense with the other securi-
ties. I believe there can be no greater or
more dangerous mistake than that. There
are many contingencies, not only in time of
war, which make it absolutely essential for us
to maintain the Cape route to India and
Australia, and I trust, therefore, that whatever
Her Majesty's Government do, there will be no
disposition to allow a false notion of economy
to interfere with the urgent duty of placing
the Cape station in a thoroughly effective
state of defence. I will now ask the noble
lord the question I have put upon the paper.

II.

Speech in the House of Lords on 13th
November, 1884.

THE EARL OF CARNARVON rose to call attention to the correspondence concerning the
defence of Colonial possessions and garrisons
abroad in reference to the recommendations
made to Her Majesty's Government by the
Royal Commission appointed to report upon
British possessions and commerce abroad.
He said:—

My lords,—I have thought it right to call
the attention of your lordships' House to this
very important matter, which has recently
attracted a good deal of the attention of the
public, and I hope my justification may be
found in the fact that, as Chairman of the

Royal Commission appointed for the defence 1884. of our foreign stations, I speak both for my- self and, to a certain extent, also for my colleagues on this question. That Commis- sion, my lords, was appointed in September, 1879. It made its first report in September, 1881, its second report early in 1882, and its last report in July, 1882. Two or three times in private I have pressed the matter upon the attention of my noble friend the First Lord of the Admiralty, and, I think, of other members of Her Majesty's Govern- ment, and in May of last year in public I earnestly urged upon Her Majesty's Govern- ment the risk of any further delay, and the great importance of dealing thoroughly with this question.

My lords, I hardly know what course I should have taken, but for the appearance a few weeks since of a short Parliamentary paper, in which it was proposed to expend a certain sum of money upon the fortification

1884. of British coaling stations abroad. I must
say I should have been guilty, I think, of a
breach of public trust if, as Chairman of that
Commission, I did not. for my own part at all
events, disclaim all responsibility for the proposals now made by the Treasury in this
paper; and if I did not say that, in my
humble opinion, the estimate of work to be
done is indeed wholly below the needs of the
case, and, in one word, illusory.

In approaching the subject, my lords, I am
beset by two difficulties; the first of which
is, that within the last few hours, I may say,
a second paper upon the same subject has
been laid before the House. Through the
courtesy of my noble friend opposite I was
allowed a sight of it yesterday, and, therefore, though I have not had time to examine
it very carefully, I think I am generally
aware of the modifications it introduces.
That paper is very embarrassing to me in
dealing with this question. In the first place

it involves a considerable change, I am 1884. willing to admit an important change, in one respect; but one that I cannot look upon as important in another respect. That paper makes an important change, because it contains a public retractation by the Treasury of the extraordinary doctrine which it had laid down in the first paper. Since the first paper was published the War Office remonstrated against the Treasury view, and thanks to that remonstrance, and thanks, I am bound to say, to a great extent to public criticism, the Treasury has seen that it could not possibly stand by the ground originally taken up.

In order to make myself clear, I had better, I think, point out to the House in a few words what is the substance of these two papers. The first paper, which has been for many weeks before the public, begins with a letter from the War Office to the Colonial Office of the 19th of March. It

1884. is, therefore, some months old, and contains first of all an estimate, from the Inspector General of Fortifications, of works and harbours which it is proposed to execute in certain stations and in certain cases therein specified. My lords, these stations are Aden, Ceylon, Singapore, Hong Kong, Sierra Leone, St. Helena, Cape of Good Hope, the Mauritius, Jamaica, and St. Lucia; and the Inspector General estimates that the works at these stations will cost in the aggregate £560,000, and the armaments £331,000, or a total of £891,000. In the next place it will be seen from the official correspondence that the estimate is based upon the report of the Royal Commission, and assumes to represent the views of that body. Now, my lords, as the correspondence proceeds, the War Office first suggests Singapore and Hong Kong as two points to be fortified, and subsequently Simon's Bay enters into their view, as also does Aden, while I am sorry to say that Table Bay practically disappears. The 1884. correspondence then winds up by the Treasury agreeing that Aden, Singapore, and Hong Kong should be dealt with at a cost of £345,000 out of the £891,000 originally proposed, naming, at the same time, no time for the completion of these works, and in a most remarkable sentence proposing to postpone the completion of the armaments, "as no expenditure need be incurred for them until the works have been completed." At present I make no comments upon this.

The second paper, which has only within the last few hours been laid upon the table, is a very remarkable corollary to that I have just quoted. It commences with a letter from the War Office of the 1st of November, which proposes certain modifications in the original estimate; first of all, a general increase on the whole sum of £18,000. The first proposal was £891,000; the present proposal is £909,000. But there is a special increase in

I.D.   C

1884. the vote for armaments, and that special increase amounts to no less than £117,000. But, my lords, that increase is purchased by a reduction of £97,000 upon the works, the first proposal for the works being £560,000, and the second £463,000, showing a reduction of £97,000. The War Office then proceeds to recommend that the armaments should not be postponed until the completion of the works, and further proposes to deal with several more stations than was originally contemplated by the Treasury, including Aden, Trincomalee, Singapore, Hong Kong, and Simon's Bay, advising that the work should be completed within the space of three years. The whole correspondence is wound up by the remarkable retractation by the Treasury of the doctrine it had originally advanced that the armaments should be postponed.

That is the state of the case as it is before the public in these two very important Parliamentary papers. As I have said before, there

is a certain improvement effected by the second 1884.
paper. I rejoice, for my own part, that the
Treasury has become so amenable to public
criticism, and I should rejoice still more if this
were the first of several steps taken in the same
direction.

My second difficulty is a greater one, and it
is this. The Commission over which I had
the honour to preside was of a strictly confidential nature, and evidence was given to us on
the distinct understanding that it should never
be published, and a great deal that we ourselves
stated and recommended was also of the same
character. At the same time, I find it extremely difficult to discuss a Parliamentary
paper such as this without alluding to the views
which the Commission held. It seems to me
that it would have been very fair had I been
allowed to give simply what I may call the
corresponding and comparative figures to those
given by the Government; for instance, that
where the Government, the War Office, or

1884. the Treasury recommended a certain sum, say £100,000, I should have been at liberty to say that in that same case the Commission stated that £200,000 or £300,000 ought to be expended. I cannot see that any unfairness or injury whatever would have accrued to the public service by such a course. But the First Lord of the Admiralty appealed to me the other night not to use one single figure out of that report, and to treat the report from first to last as an absolute secret. I earnestly hope that my noble friend and other Cabinet Ministers are themselves as careful as they can be in their custody of these confidential papers, for it has been my fortune several times to become aware that papers of the highest importance, both on military and foreign affairs, have found their way into the possession of foreign Governments. I do not know where the fault has been, but I know that matters of extreme, of vital importance, have leaked out, and found their way into other hands. I think

it would have been fair had I been allowed to
make a comparative statement on this occa-
sion, but when the report of a Commission is
confidential, and when the Government asks
one to treat the document as secret, one is
bound to accept that view, and I do accept it;
but in arguing this case I am greatly fettered
and restrained, and I shall find it very difficult
indeed to make my case clear, dealing, as I
shall be obliged to do, with generalities, instead
of with the few explicit figures which would
have at once carried conviction. With these
explanations, I will proceed to the subject in
hand.

First of all, as regards the dates of this
correspondence some comments have been
made out of doors. There was a long delay
between March 19th, when the first letter was
written, and August 12th, when the last was
written, if it be the last. But the great fault
that I find with respect to chronology is in
this, that three precious years have been

1884. allowed to go by since the first report of the Commissioners was presented to the Government, and that two years have been allowed to pass since the presentation of the last report. Now, one word as to the order in which these stations are taken. In the first paper Aden, Singapore, and Hong Kong were the three stations chosen for these works, and in the second paper Ceylon is added and Simon's Bay. I could say something about the choice of Trincomalee, but I will leave that matter to the responsibility of the First Lord of the Admiralty and his colleagues. So two stations have been added, Trincomalee and Simon's Bay. The place which one would think would be the very first point to be defended was ignored in the first paper. The Commissioners said that the defence of the Cape was of essential, vital, and primary importance, and if the First Lord of the Admiralty will refer to the reports that were issued he will appreciate the weight of my remarks.

Let me remind your lordships what the 1884.
Cape really is to us. First of all, it is the
central point on the alternative route to the
Suez route, and more than that, it will be
the only route to our Eastern possessions if the
Suez route should ever be blocked; and he
would be a very bold man indeed who did
not contemplate the contingency of that route
being blocked should a European war arise.
Secondly, we have to consider how very large
a stake we have commercially in that route.
Five years ago the commerce that went round
and touched the Cape was represented by
£90,000,000 yearly, while that which went
through the Suez Canal was represented by
£65,000,000. The commerce that might have
to pass the Cape in time of war may now
amount to £200,000,000. Now, in the last
Parliamentary paper, it is proposed to fortify
Simon's Bay alone, and no mention is made
of Table Bay. But the two places are so
dependent on each other that to fortify

1884. Simon's Bay without fortifying Table Bay also would be to leave your back door open to the foe, and to have only half the fortifications which you ought to have. This has never been controverted or denied. It is said in this paper that the interests which we have at the Cape are confined to Simon's Bay, and that at Table Bay there are only Colonial interests. That is a most extraordinary statement. It is also alleged in this paper that you may leave the fortification of Table Bay to the Colonial Government; but any one who knows the views of the Colonial Government is aware that it is idle to think that the Cape Government will undertake the task. They will co-operate with you by giving valuable land and spending a comparatively considerable sum of money, but anything more than that we cannot expect from them, nor do I think we have a right to expect more.

Having disposed of the question of the

Cape, in order to illustrate the way in which 1884. the matter has been treated by the Treasury, I now proceed to the consideration of the subject generally. What is it we have to defend? The question must be considered under the four heads of our great Colonies, our smaller Colonies, our trade afloat, our coaling and other imperial military stations. As regards our great Colonies, we ought to be called upon to do very little indeed. Australia has set an admirable example, their public-spirited and generous expenditure of public money having, I trust, placed Melbourne and Sydney in a position of almost confident security. As regards most of our smaller Colonies, they are defensible so long as we maintain the supremacy of the sea and no longer. As regards the trade afloat, it was calculated four or five years ago, and I have no doubt the figures have increased, that £900,000,000 sterling represented the commerce of this country which annually crossed the seas, and that

1884. £150,000,000 represented the commerce that was afloat at any given time. Now I come to the question of imperial fortresses and coaling stations. In time of peace the Admiralty have about fifty stations upon which they can depend for coaling, but of these the greater number are in foreign countries; and I need not remind your lordships that in time of war coaling stations belonging to belligerents or neutrals would be shut against us. There remain the four great stations which I may call the maritime quadrilateral of England —namely, Gibraltar and Malta in the Mediterranean, and Bermuda and Halifax on the other side of the Atlantic. Those four great stations have for many years past been the special care of Her Majesty's Government. They were remitted to the Commission, but about a year and a half after we had commenced our investigations they were withdrawn from our cognisance, and, therefore, it is impossible for me to express any opinion with respect to them. But I do say that, when 1884. Her Majesty's Government removed these four stations, which formed a maritime quadrilateral, from our cognisance, they assumed a weighty responsibility, and are bound all the more to take the necessary steps for their defence. I hope that the defences are adequate, but the responsibility in this case must rest with the Government.

There remain after this deduction something like sixteen or seventeen coaling stations abroad, some of greater, some of less consequence. Now, what is the value of those stations? because out of doors I very often notice a most singular ignorance on the subject. Those stations I hold to be vital to us in time of war. Steam has revolutionised all the conditions of modern warfare, especially in ships of war. My noble friend knows very well that the amount of coal a warship can carry is comparatively very small, and coal is to a modern ship of war what sails were to

1884. a wooden three-decker in the time of Nelson. If you allow your ships to be deprived of coal they will lie useless on the water. In the old days the wooden ships might be repaired by the ship's carpenter after a general action, but your iron ships must go to places where there are docks and means by which they can be properly repaired. At the principal of those coaling stations there are the facilities which would enable the refitting to be undertaken. But it is absolutely necessary to defend those places, and if you leave them exposed you leave them to be taken possession of by the enemy. It will not do to defend them merely by ships of war, because if ships of war are to watch over the coaling stations in which those valuable stores are deposited, they are tied to particular points of the coast, and they cannot operate generally with effect against the enemy. It is necessary, as this report states, to defend your coaling stations against the heaviest guns and artillery. You cannot have 1884. very slight works, because during the last few years the calibre of the guns has so much increased that you must now count on ships with six inches or eight inches of armour; and this involves both a considerable increase in the solidity of the works and the range of their armaments.

I have seen it stated of late that an alternative is to be found in the increase of the Navy. That is a total mistake, for the reasons I have already stated. If you have no place at which your ships can adequately re-fit and re-coal you must double and treble your ships, and they may even then be perfectly useless. Therefore, it is for the Government to determine what the coaling and refitting stations should be, and then adequately to provide for their defence. England has, undoubtedly, more and better stations abroad than any other great European power. How if those stations are undefended? Instead of

1884. being a source of strength in time of war they become a distinct source of weakness. I shall wind up this part of the case by reminding your lordships that upon that question depends, not only the keeping afloat of Her Majesty's Navy, but the whole maintenance of the trade of this country; and, inasmuch as the life of this country is commerce, our national existence itself may be said to depend on the number of our well-defended stations.

Now I come to the proposals which Her Majesty's Government and the Treasury have made. I cannot compare these proposals with the recommendations which the Commission made. And here arises one of the great difficulties under which I labour. I must not contrast the proposals which the Government make with those of the Commission, but I may surely give this as my opinion—that the scheme ought to be a whole and complete scheme, and by that I mean that there should be works both for land and sea defence. I may 1884. observe, in passing, that I am at a loss to understand whether in this estimate of the War Office it is land works or sea works that are meant, or whether both are included. I hope my noble friend, when he speaks, will throw some light on this subject. But whether sea works or land works, they ought to be supplemented by mines or torpedoes and other defences of that kind.

I next approach the question of expenditure. The land and sea works and the other separate matters dealt with in the first Parliamentary paper fall very much below what I consider satisfactory. If I were to say that they ought at least to be doubled, I should not be going at all beyond the truth. It must be remembered that there is no provision made for these supplementary items to which I have just alluded. I read the other day a speech made by Sir Thomas Brassey, in which he dealt with the question of the Navy. Sir

1884. Thomas Brassey was one of the original members of the Commission, and I wish very much that he had remained to the end upon it. His loss was a great loss to us, and it was still greater as he was removed at the time when we came to consider the subject as a whole. Sir Thomas Brassey, speaking lately for the Government, used these words: " The protecting of our coaling stations is another matter of urgency, and the correspondence lately published will show that the Government are alive to the requirements of the Empire, and have made proper arrangements for the commencement of the work." When I come to contrast these words of Sir Thomas Brassey with the proposals, it will be seen that there is a great *hiatus.* Take the first paper. The Treasury is the governing spirit in the matter, and therefore I must speak of the paper as the Treasury paper. The Treasury allows for the expenditure £891,000. I consider that sum to be far below the requirements of the case. The next step, and it is a very ingenious one, is to reduce the sum of £891,000 to £345,000. How is that done? It is done by striking out the majority of the places that are to be fortified, and naming Aden, the Straits, and Hong Kong, as being the most urgent. No doubt those three places are extremely important stations, but, unless the Government have before their eyes the danger of an Eastern war, I do not think they are the most important in the order of priority. I do not see what there is to justify the Government in assuming that those stations are the most important. The fact is, they are the richest, and larger local contributions can be obtained from them than from other places.

But the estimate is subject to a further reduction. The £345,000 is brought down to £150,000 by the separation of local and Imperial charges. The local charges are set down at £195,000 and the Imperial at £150,000.

I.D.   D

1884. That is not all. The sum of £150,000 again, by a most ingenious process of arithmetic, is reduced to £47,000, the division being—armaments, £103,750; works, £47,000. The Treasury then winds up by postponing the armaments until the works are completed, and by informing us that the Indian Government had undertaken to advance the £47,000, or something like that sum. Thus it is said, that little, if any, charge will fall on the Army votes this year, and it will be certainly un-necessary to present a supplementary estimate this Session. I have come to this conclusion—that, whatever the expenditure of the Government in this matter may be on paper, in prac-tice it will be found to be nil. This shows the spirit in which the whole of the proposal is conceived, and what vital injury will be done to the country if the Treasury is allowed to overrule and overbear the action of those departments which are responsible for the safety of the country abroad. Let me say on that point that the Commissioners framed 1884. their estimates upon the lowest possible scale, and my own feeling and that of some of my colleagues was that if we erred it was in recommending an insufficient sum for the defence of these places. Let me explain how we arrived at our estimates. We framed them first of all upon data supplied to us from the Office of the Inspector-General of Fortifications, from the War Office and from the Admiralty. We subjected the figures to the closest scrutiny, and sent out the estimates to be verified by local committees on the spot. We also sent out most experienced naval and military officers to test the accuracy of the estimates. I should like to know upon what data the Treasury, the War Office, and the Admiralty are proceeding in this case, and how the different views of the War Office three years ago and at present are reconciled. In the next place, the Commission endeavoured to look at the scheme as a whole, but this

1884. scheme which is now before us is conceived in as narrow and departmental a spirit as any I have yet seen. We rescued many separate questions from the departmental mode of treatment, and for the first time we obtained a certain concentration of official knowledge and communication. It was my earnest hope that that state of things would continue, and that some means would be adopted to prevent the terrible complications which arise from the offices corresponding separately and individually with one another. To my deep regret and sorrow such has not been the case, and I see from this paper that you are working under a most unsatisfactory system. I am satisfied that until some such system as I have indicated is adopted this country will not be in the position in which it ought to be as regards the consideration of questions of defence.

The word "garrisons" is mentioned in the title of this Parliamentary paper, but it is the beginning and the end, for we hear nothing 1884. further about garrisons. As to that, the Commission recommended concentration of troops for this purpose, and I hoped and believed that this part of our recommendations would be carried out; but this is not the case, and I am bound to say that, in my humble opinion, the existing garrisons in some parts of the world are inadequate, although no doubt much has been done by means of local contributions. Of one thing I am sure, and that is, that this question of garrisons cannot be separated from the question of fortifications. It is a question which the Government must face.

There remains the question of armaments, which may be considered from three points of view—the number of guns, their weight, and their cost. If I look at the first of these Parliamentary papers, I can only say that the armaments are, like the works, singularly insufficient and below the mark. I find

1884. that, while the proposed number of medium and light guns was somewhat below that which it should have been, the real deficiency occurred in the class of heavy guns; and I need not point out that in time of war it is upon the heavy guns that you must depend in fortifications. In the second paper, this item is far more satisfactory, but at the same time, as far as I can judge, the estimate is too low. I am very much afraid that the guns on which you are to depend are very much in arrear. You have to provide for the Navy, for home fortifications, and for foreign stations. The Navy is not yet supplied, and on the home fortifications many of the guns are of an old type, and are virtually useless.

The real difficulty is—and it is well that Parliament should know it — that we have not plant adequate to turn out the number of guns we need. We are dependent upon Sir Joseph Whitworth for the steel for the heavier guns, and I believe the best gunpowder is imported from Germany, and is 1884. produced by a process which is a secret and a monopoly. Can anything be more anomalous than that this country should be in such a position? Some guns can be manufactured in a year and some require three years, so that the average time required is about two years. Yet the Treasury actually proposes to defer dealing with armaments until the works are completed. If the Treasury thinks we could turn out the guns we should want as soon as a war broke out, one can only marvel at such an opinion.

There are many proposals subsidiary to those to which I have alluded which the Commissioners thought it their bounden duty to bring under the attention of the Government, and I hope that they have had a somewhat larger consideration than has been accorded to other recommendations in the Inspector-General's office. May I call to mind the composition of that Commission? It was composed of

1884. very representative men. We examined witnesses of every class and kind—the highest military, naval, commercial, and scientific authorities, including the illustrious Duke at the head of the Army, the First Lord of the Admiralty, and the highest military and naval officers. There was not a single branch of knowledge, science, or information that could be brought to bear on the question that was not appealed to in the course of the inquiry. We sat for three years; we did not shrink from any amount of work; and we only discharged our consciences in saying anything that was calculated to awaken anxiety in the minds of the Government. Therefore it is with regret that I see the outcome in the Treasury letter. I know what the Treasury is. No doubt it is a valuable office in restricting extravagance and keeping accounts, but it has no special knowledge on questions of this kind. If the responsible heads of a great department like the Navy allow the Treasury

to come in and overbear their deliberate judg- 1884.
ment by mere penny-wise considerations, they
incur a great responsibility.

The position seems to me to be by no
means satisfactory. On the one hand, we have,
first of all, these four great fortresses to which
I have alluded. I hope they are adequately and
fully defended. We have sixteen or seventeen
others that are very inadequately defended, or
not defended at all. We have inadequate garrisons. We have at many points no works
worth speaking of. We have no guns worth
speaking of. Our lines of commercial steamers
are not duly guarded, and we have no security
that in time of war our food supply will be
safe. There is everything which, under a few
adverse conditions, might easily lead to a great
national disaster. On the other hand, what are
the proposals with which this state of things
is met ? The coaling stations are dismissed.
There is no provision made for barracks or
for any of the essential secondary supplements

1884. of the existing works, which, in my opinion, are much below efficiency. Even the armaments to be provided will be still below the mark. It is impossible not to feel extremely anxious that the Government should not in a case of this kind be influenced by considerations of parsimony, and should not hesitate to look the facts in the face. I have no wish to say a word to produce a panic. The proof of that is, that, for three years since the report of this Commission was presented, I have waited patiently, giving only a few occasional indications of my opinion to my noble friend opposite and to the Government generally. I hope I have said nothing from a party point of view. I should scorn to initiate a discussion on a question of this sort on party lines. It is my conscientious belief that I have said less than the case really requires. I, for one, refuse all further responsibility in this matter. I personally wash my hands of whatever liability there may be attaching to me or

any other member of the Commission. I have 1884.
spoken my mind fairly and fully; not so
much so as I could have done, but yet sufficiently for my purpose. My object is to warn
the Government that the present state of the
defences is inadequate and unsatisfactory, and
that when any untoward or unfavourable
circumstances occur the vital interests of the
country may be placed in serious jeopardy.

III.

Speech in the House of Lords on 16th March, 1885.

THE EARL OF CARNARVON said :—

My noble friend may congratulate himself upon having elicited a very important statement, which was well worthy the attention of the House, and your lordships will read the papers moved for with very great interest, because I understand that many applications have been made for them, and that they will show what it is the Colonies want, and what the Government are willing to do. It seems to me, however, from the statement of the noble earl opposite, that the whole burden of initiating a colonial naval force has been thrown upon the Colonies instead of Her Majesty's Government taking it upon themselves. It is in the memory of many members of this House that some few years ago an Act was passed for the purpose of establishing a colonial navy, and it is a question of no small interest why that Act has failed to answer the expectations of those who desired that it should be passed. That Act has, however, failed both to secure that amount of naval discipline which is desirable and necessary in a colonial force, and to bring such force into close connection with the British Navy.

One objection was that the Australian Colonies were either unwilling or, at all events, unprepared to accept joint liability for the defence of the Empire. The facts have disproved this, and there can now be no doubt as to what the disposition of the Colonies is. But there is also another objection which claims great consideration, and that is that Australian ships must never be removed from Australia for Imperial purposes. I am bound to say there is great reason in that objection. My own view, however, is, first, that they should be able to secure that any ship or ships provided by Australian expen-

1885. diture should be maintained on the Australian
coast; and secondly, that those ships should
be brought into connection with the Imperial
naval force, and where practicable inter-
changed, so becoming part and parcel of the
general naval forces of the Empire. I am,
indeed, disposed to go a step beyond my noble
friend. I think there would be no harm in
arranging that every Australian officer in the
Australian naval service should directly hold
the Queen's commission. Secondly, that we
should give to the Australian Government or
Colony the same number of commissions as
would be represented by the ships which they
establish and maintain. These ships should
be placed—and I would admit of no compromise on this point—under the direct control of
the English Admiralty. Nothing short of this
will secure the incorporation which we wish
to see effected between the colonial and home
naval forces of this country. Ordinarily these
colonial ships should be maintained on the
colonial station, but they should be rendered

available and interchangeable in time of ex- 1885.
treme peril. It has been my lot to watch the
growth of feeling in the Colonies on this subject. In 1878 I made proposals to these great
Colonies with regard to incurring joint liability
with the Mother Country in various matters,
and among others in naval matters; and if my
proposal had been adopted much of the trouble
which has since arisen in the South Pacific
would have been prevented. Still later I was
chairman of a colonial commission, and there
was then much more practical co-operation
than before. That was four or five years ago.
Since then we have advanced nearer to a
common ground. I deprecate the conduct
of the Government in not taking the initiative
in this matter, and I sincerely trust that the
result of the more recent communications
between the Imperial Government and the
Colonies will be to further advance that most
desirable of objects — a closer co-operation
between the great self-governing Colonies and
the Mother Country.

IV.

THE ABANDONMENT OF PORT HAMILTON

Letter to the Editor of the "Times," 13th December, 1886.

SIR,—It is reported that we intend to cede Port Hamilton to China on condition that China allows no other Power to acquire it.

I confess to some regret at this announcement, if it is correct. I am well aware of the inexpediency, whether as regards the expense of garrisons or the difficulty of furnishing them, of holding more military outposts than are absolutely necessary; and probably few Englishmen have much notion of where or what Port Hamilton is. Nevertheless, it has a real value. It is one of those positions which may be described as keys, governing the conditions of naval attack and defence in the China seas. It is not, like the Russian 1886. Vladivostock, frozen up for some months in every year; it possesses a magnificent harbour; it is so naturally defensible that it has been called a Chinese Gibraltar; it is, in fact, almost necessary for attack, if attack ever becomes expedient, and it is equally important for the protection of trade in the event of war. In other words, the masters of Port Hamilton are masters of all that lies between Russian territory in the north and Hong Kong, about 1,200 miles to the south. There are, indeed, coaling depôts at Shanghai, Nagasaki, and Yokohama, but it must be remembered that they are undefended, and are not on English soil. They cannot, therefore, be depended upon in time of war. But if these coaling stations cannot be maintained, the whole of our large trade north of Hong Kong would have to be abandoned.

This is not problematical. The most competent experts and the highest naval authorities

1886. on the spot have repeatedly affirmed it ; and till Port Hamilton was quite recently acquired, the Admiralty never ceased to pray for its acquisition. Have they now changed their minds, and if so, on what grounds ? During the Russian war—whatever may be the value of the analogy—we found it necessary to occupy Gothland with the consent of Sweden. Could we count upon a similar permission of China in the event of another Russian war ?

It is said that we are ceding this position to China on the understanding that she will not transfer it to any other Power ; but what security have we that she can observe that condition ? For years past, with patient assiduity, Russia has been working her way southwards to "open water" in the extreme east, as in the Mediterranean ; is it wise to place in doubtful keeping a military position which can govern all naval, and consequently all trade, operations in these seas ?

Much may be said, and reasonably, against

retaining such positions as Port Hamilton 1886
unless they are fortified and garrisoned; but it
must be remembered that so long as the English flag and a corporal's guard are there they
cannot be taken from us without open quarrel.
When, however, they are in other hands—no
matter what assurances and conditions—the
case is very different. If Port Hamilton had
never been acquired by us, there might be
somewhat to say against our taking it, both
on general grounds and in reference to our
particular relations with China, Japan, Corea
and Russia. But we must assume that all
these considerations were carefully weighed
when it was decided to hoist the English flag
in Port Hamilton. I hope that the reversal
of that decision by the Admiralty has been
equally well considered.

I remain, Sir,

Your obedient Servant,

CARNARVON.

LONDON, *December* 11*th*, 1886.

E 2

V.

THE DEFENCE OF OUR COALING STATIONS AND COMMERCIAL PORTS.

Letter to the Editor of the " Times," Thursday,
January 6th, 1887.

SIR,—Though we wait for explanations of
the resignation of the late Chancellor of the
Exchequer,* yet sufficient has transpired to
make it clear that the defence of our coaling
stations abroad and of our commercial ports
at home is involved in the controversy. So
very grave does this question appear to me,
that with your leave I would make some
observations on it ; and if it be thought
beyond the province of a civilian to speak
confidently on a subject into which so many
professional considerations enter, I can only
reply that I was for three years chairman of

* Lord Randolph Churchill.

the Commission for the Defence of the British 1887.
Possessions and Commerce Abroad, and that
I have spared neither time nor trouble in
forming an independent opinion. I omit now
all reference to the defence of the home ports
or of the Imperial fortresses of Gibraltar,
Malta, Halifax, and Bermuda, and I confine
myself to the coaling stations.

The Commission were unanimously agreed
on two main points at least—first, the extreme
peril to our Navy and our commerce from
leaving those stations undefended ; secondly, as
to the general mode of that defence. As regards
this last point, they made various recommendations, and they estimated the cost of the
necessary defences at a very reasonable figure.
It is, of course, impossible to enter upon the
details of a confidential document ; but I may
say that, as far as I know, our recommendations have substantially stood the test of professional criticism, and have in the main secured
the assent of successive Governments, even

those which were most anxious to distinguish themselves by military and naval economy. Mr. Gladstone's Government of 1884, Lord Salisbury's of 1885, Mr. Gladstone's of 1886, have all unreservedly pledged themselves in principle to the necessity—I shall not go too far if I say vital necessity—of these defences. For in truth it is nothing less. Coal has become the most potent factor in the arithmetic of naval war. Without it, our foreign commerce and our vast carrying trade cease to exist; without it, our ships of war can neither fight nor move; and, even with it, there is no security, unless it is adequately protected, for it becomes the prey of the first hostile cruiser.

On the other hand, our Empire, scattered as it is, has this advantage—that we hold a succession of defensible points, where our ships can find ports in which to coal, to refit, to repair, whence the great lines of commercial communication can be patrolled or guarded, and where a base of operations against an enemy can be secured. Further, the defence 1887. of these positions means not only all these advantages to us, but the loss of them to our foes; and therefore those stations are in one sense almost as necessary as ships or guns, for without them ships and guns may easily be rendered useless. Our insular position has hitherto relieved us from the burden of maintaining armies on an European scale; but our continental neighbours are no longer content with a military predominance on land. The maritime rivalry of France is, to say the least, very serious; and while we grudge a few hundred thousand pounds for the defence of our coaling stations, France has commenced an estimated expenditure of £3,000,000 on one alone of her foreign outposts. I need not, however, enlarge on this, for I do not believe that there is any competent judge who will dispute my statement.

Now of these coaling stations, while all are important, some are more important than

1887. others, and while some are being fortified by the voluntary efforts of our great self-governing Colonies, others must almost entirely depend upon the action of the Imperial Government. It is rather a complicated question. The Australasian Colonies have done much for themselves, and the fortifications of Sydney and Melbourne, while essential to the safety of those great towns, also secure for the Queen's ships coals and arsenals and all that gives life and power to a fleet. No call is, therefore, made on us here, nor are we required to pay one shilling for the enjoyment of these advantages. But there are other stations which are necessary for the protection of our commerce—such as Hong Kong, Singapore, Aden—and the mercantile communities which have sprung up in some of these places are able and willing to bear their share of the expense. Roughly speaking, the agreement is that they should provide the works, and that the Home Government should furnish the armaments; and it generally happens that the Government is the last to complete its part of the bargain. In the present instance the highest praise is due to Hong Kong and Singapore. The one has, I believe, spent more than £100,000, the other nearly that sum, upon their respective works; but the Imperial contribution of guns is still wanting in Singapore.

Progress, therefore, has been made at these and some other places, though mostly at the expense of the local communities; but with a strange procrastination the effective defence of the Cape, by far our most important station, has been left neglected, and even its details are as yet undecided. As far as I can understand the case, the Cape Government have some just cause of complaint for the manner in which their overtures have been met; for while unable, like their richer fellow-subjects in Australia, to undertake the entire defence of their principal port, they have, though mainly Dutch in their extraction, shown no unwillingness to bear a reasonable share in

1887. the work. Be this, however, as it may, the Cape is the great halfway house between England and the East, and as an alternative to the Suez route is, perhaps, even of more importance to us than all the other stations which we own. So important did the Commission consider it that they postponed all other considerations to report upon it at once, and to urge on the Government immediate action. That recommendation was made in September, 1881, and we are now in January, 1887. Something, indeed, has been done, but unless supplemented by something else, that " something," in a military sense, is worth nothing. Cape Town is like a house with two doors, and it is useless to close one if the other is left open to an enemy. Simon's Bay, on the west of the peninsula, is the one; Table Bay, that magnificent spot so familiar to Eastern-bound travellers, is the other. Simon's Bay, which is used by the Admiralty as a convenient anchorage, is now fairly defended at Imperial cost for purely Imperial 1887. purposes, but Table Bay and Cape Town are without a vestige of protection. On the shores of that Bay colonial and commercial enterprise have been busy. Large floating basins and jetties, a fine breakwater, a graving dock, workshops, coal stores, with appliances for coaling and repairing, have sprung into exist-ence—an instalment only, I trust, of the still larger works of the future. Yet this great creation, a source of wealth and prosperity in peace and a priceless resource in time of war, lies during some temporary absence of our fleet at the mercy of a single cruiser.

I have spoken only of the Cape, and I have singled it out as an illustration, though the most important one, of the whole question; but when I state that a period of about two years is required from the ordering of a gun of the new type to its delivery abroad, and when I add that—so far as I know—nothing has yet been decided as to the apportionment

1887. of the cost of the Cape Town armament or of the works which must be constructed to hold that armament, I think you will agree with me that not another day of delay should be added to the long term of fruitless debate which has elapsed. In 1878, under the panic of Russian hostilities, a few earthworks were hastily constructed at the Cape, and some guns were despatched. But the hot fit passed, the cold succeeded; the temporary defences have become useless in the altered conditions of modern gunnery, and only exist as a monument of Imperial inefficiency and waste.

I will not here inquire into the causes of this delay,—whether the excessive pressure of business on a Minister, or the conflict of departments, or the natural desire of the Treasury to measure public requirements by the sole measure of arithmetic, or the tendency to subordinate distant objects, however important, to near objects, however small, or the almost hopeless difficulty under our Parlia-

mentary system of providing the necessary 1887.
means if they are borne on the annual
estimates, I will not here argue. One thing
only is clear, that decision and action ought
long before this to have been taken. My own
conscience, at least, is clear. I have repeatedly, in public and private, urged the insanity
of allowing a further continuance of this
dangerous state, and now when, as we understand, the Government is impugned for a
desire to remedy it, I should at least feel
myself guilty if I did not in the strongest
language that I can command bear witness
to the necessity of action, and if I did not give
them on such a subject whatever support is
in my power.

I remain, Sir,

Your obedient Servant,

CARNARVON.

43, PORTMAN SQUARE, *January 5th,* 1887.

VI.

THE DEFENCE OF OUR COMMERCIAL PORTS.

Letter to the Editor of the "Times," January 8th, 1887.

SIR,—In my last letter I dwelt upon the vital importance to us of our coaling stations abroad, but the defence of our home ports is so intimately connected with them that some further observations seem necessary to conclude the case.

Of the commercial value represented by the trade of those ports I need make no estimate. Up and down the Humber, the Tyne, the Tees, the Clyde, the Firth of Forth, and the Mersey there passes a volume of wealth which—London only excepted—exceeds all that the world has ever seen within so narrow a compass. Yet the great towns which these rivers command are almost defenceless. Without discussing the

risks of an actual landing—a separate question 1887.
—a few hostile cruisers could in the temporary
absence of our fleet bombard or lay them under
contribution. There are few works, no floating defences, no armaments worth mentioning,
except a few old-pattern 38-ton guns at Liverpool; and though there is a fair proportion of
submarine mines there is a total absence of all
systematic defence. Let me add to this, in
passing, that the position of our arsenals and
dockyards, on which our existence may depend,
is not much more satisfactory. The fortifications are either incomplete or in a great measure
obsolete; the armaments are of the old type;
the garrisons are not real garrisons in the full
sense of the term, where every man knows his
place, and all are trained to the requirements
of sudden war; and the whole defence is wanting in many of those things which competent
judges rightly call essentials.

I would not be understood to overlook
some recent improvements, or the value of such

1887. experiments as the attack on Milford Haven, but at the best those are makeshifts and feeble palliatives, bearing no kind of proportion to the real exigencies of the case.

Most serious of all is the question of fortifications and guns; for in both cases time is needed to correct our deficiencies, and in both a real revolution has taken place during the last few years. As is well known, the granite and concrete defences are no longer of value unless they are coated with enormously heavy iron or steel or compound armour, and even thus they cannot cope with modern artillery. Change, too, begets change. Not only the construction, but the character and disposition of our fortifications are undergoing alteration, and we are reverting in theory to the earthworks of former days, though built and arranged on new principles. I say reverting in theory, for unhappily we are a long way removed from practice, and according to our usual wont are at present only engaged in talking of what should be done; but over and above this, to make an immediate and extensive alteration in this respect would involve far too large an outlay. We can only work towards our object cautiously and as opportunity presents itself.

But the question of guns is different. Immediate action there is possible and within reasonable limits of expenditure. It was the duty of the Commission of which I was chairman to inquire into the then imminent revolution in the construction of our guns, and we anticipated and recommended the great change which has actually taken effect during the last five years. The result has justified us, and the new type of gun, which we so strongly urged upon the Government, is now recognised as the only reliable armament in the attack or defence of first-class positions. A length of range and an accuracy of fire which a few years since would have been deemed fabulous, under the control and direction of the most beautiful application of

I.D.   F

1887. science are now attained.   It is true that in their elaborate mountings and machinery such guns combine the disadvantages of slowness of manufacture, delicacy of construction, shortness of life, and great costliness.   But a good article is generally expensive; and if such guns contribute materially to the public safety they are in the long run cheap.   Moreover, a smaller number of them will, under our new system of defence, do the work of a much larger number under the old conditions.   But be the number what it may, we have no choice in the matter.   These costly but effective weapons will decide modern wars and the fate of nations; and yet, marvellous to say, we have not one of them in our home ports, nor have we even one first-class one mounted in any arsenal or dockyard.

I write of course as a civilian, pretending to no technical knowledge, and I seek to confine my remarks to indisputable facts and arguments of which any civilian of ordinary intelligence can judge. But I am confident 1887. that what I have now said is substantially correct, and if so, I think that the most urgent measures of reform may be briefly thus summed up :—

1. The manufacture of the new armament should be pressed forward with the least possible delay, and this is the policy, both as regards coaling stations and home ports, which was laid down in 1884 by the then Secretary of State. Many guns, indeed, of the old pattern may, for the purpose of high-angle fire, be economically converted and used for coast defence, but an immediate supply of the new guns is imperative.

2. The defensive works of the great commercial ports should no longer be delayed. It is madness to leave them to the sole protec᷂ tion of submarine mines, without the support of land batteries and unaided by floating defences.

3. But works are useless without men to

1887. hold them; and in the absence of regular troops an effective organisation of volunteer artillery seems the obvious if not the only alternative. Such an organisation presents no insuperable difficulties. In most of our northern towns there is an abundance of men of the right class and of public spirit. The experiment has already been tried with success, though on far too limited a scale; and all that is needed for its full development is some moderate compensation for loss of time. The same support which has been wisely given to volunteer submarine miners might be extended to volunteer artillerymen.

4. Some subsidiary re-organisation of our general defensive arrangements is certainly necessary. For the sake of illustration, what can be more fatal to rapid and effective action in times of emergency than some of the military districts into which the country is divided, as where Plymouth, Falmouth, and Milford are placed under a single commander; or where

the Humber, the Tees, the Tyne, and the 1887.
Mersey are under the charge of another, who,
I believe, resides in York? There may originally have been reasons for such an arrangement, but in the complex and scientific tactics
of the future it must stand utterly condemned.
The management of the new class of batteries,
with their scientific apparatus, of the heavy
guns, of the machine guns, of the torpedoes,
and the submarine mines, of the torpedo boats
and gunboats, of the floating defences and
electric lights—in a word, of the hundred and
one agencies, scientific and mechanical, which
none but an expert can remember or describe,
must now be combined under one chief. On
board our great warships all individuals are
trained to work together and to concentrate
their separate duties or functions on a common
purpose ; the ship is a great scientific machine ;
but we have no corresponding combination
for the defence of our commercial ports. We
have outgrown the old system, and we are

1887. making no determined attempt to cope with the new order; we spend on things obsolete, we economise on things vital, and we seem to imagine that our past fortune is a guarantee for our future safety. If the Government are now disposed without fear or favour to do their duty, I believe they will receive the hearty support of every lover of his country.

I remain, Sir,

Your obedient Servant,

CARNARVON.

43, PORTMAN SQUARE, *January 7th*, 1887.

VII.

DEFENCE OF OUR COMMERCIAL PORTS AND COALING STATIONS.

Letter to the Editor of the "Times," 30th August, 1887.

SIR,—The Session is rapidly closing, another year has gone by, and very little progress can be reported as to the defence of our commercial ports at home, or of our coaling stations abroad. Here we have done nothing, and there we move as if we had no heart in the work. With your permission, therefore, I will once more briefly call attention to this vital question, on which the security alike of our commerce and our fleets depends.

First, as to our commercial ports. At t *r.* *r* commencement of the Session their condition, as I stated in your columns, was almost, if not quite, defenceless; and that dangerous and dis-

1887. creditable state remains unaltered. The Tyne, with the great manufactory at Elswick, the Clyde, with its great shipbuilding and refitting yards, are without protection, while the Mersey, with the wealth of Liverpool, has only the so-called defence of some old-type 38-ton guns. There is, indeed, so far as I am aware, in no commercial port a single heavy gun mounted of modern pattern. Every officer and expert of experience—worse still, every foreign Government—knows this; while the recent naval manœuvres make this at least clear — that, under conditions most favourable to defence, English ports can be surprised by a hostile fleet.

If Parliament, absorbed in every other subject under heaven except the old-fashioned duty of providing for national defence, will do nothing, then I believe that our great commercial ports would, if the matter were placed fairly before them, do much for themselves by voluntary effort. But, however this may be, it

It is simple madness in the doubtful state of European politics, and with our full knowledge of
the pitiless consequences of modern warfare, to
leave towns in which our wealth and strength
lie stored at the mercy of a daring cruiser.

Next, as to our foreign stations. They con-
sist of two classes—first, the Imperial coaling
stations where British communities have grown
up for trading and other purposes; second, the
great colonies, such as New South Wales and
Victoria, where England in all the fulness of
her race and language and institutions has
been transplanted across the seas. Let me say
a few words on each of these.

First, the Imperial coaling stations. In
many of these, such as Hong Kong, Singapore,
Mauritius, a division of expense as regards the
defences has been agreed to. The local community undertook to erect the works or to
provide the money for them, while the Imperial
Government engaged to supply the armaments.
These communities have as a rule performed

1887. their part of the contract; we have in every
case left our share unperformed, either wholly
or in part. Each of the three important
stations which I have mentioned—each essential to the protection of our vast commerce
and to the security of our fleets, each in their
different degrees essential to our supremacy in
the Eastern seas—remains unfortified, because
we have not yet sent out the armament which
we engaged to provide.

For this discreditable and dangerous condition I have sometimes heard the excuse set
up that the manufacture of modern armaments
is so slow that two years are needed for the
construction of a gun with its proper mountings. A melancholy apology! If the manufacture is so slow, the guns should have been
ordered as soon as it was known that Singapore
or Hong Kong or Mauritius was prepared to
make the works or to give the money; instead
of which, in order to save financial appearances,
and to gain a false credit for economy in the

Estimates, we have made or allowed delays in giving the necessary orders to the manufacturers. More that this — even the auxiliary armaments, those machine-guns and quick-firing guns which are absolutely necessary in modern war, which even without the heavier artillery might for purposes of defence have an almost incalculable value, and which can be procured and sent out at once, are, probably for the same reason, subjected to the same fatal delay. They have not been sent out; I might perhaps ask if they are even ordered? The fault of all this is with us. Our endless committees that too often decide nothing, our undue centralisation here, our want of proper individual responsibility there, the absence of that combination of administrative knowledge and authority, which is very graphically described by Sir James Stephen's recent Commission, are productive of delays, errors, waste, and danger in this, as in many other parts of our cumbrous system.

1887.   I will not repeat now what I have said in
former letters, nor will I say anything about
the incalculable importance of garrisons except
this—that the many different questions into
which this large subject divides itself ought
not, as is too much the case, to be considered separately.   Forts are useless without the guns; forts and guns are valueless
without the trained garrisons to put in them;
and I may add that even forts, guns, and
garrisons together are unequal to the work
of defence if they are not combined and supplemented by the scientific requirements of
modern war.   Yet such in a great measure
is our practice, and we are led into it by
that false economy—fruitful parent of public
waste—which too often suggests to Ministers
the fatal temptation of reducing estimates by
delaying the manufacture of armaments.   Thus
forts built at great cost stand useless for want
of the necessary guns, or guns are transferred to some place where they are wanted

from another place where they cannot be 1887.
spared.

Meanwhile, in contrast to those sorry shifts, some at least of our great colonies across the sea, taking a truer measure of public duties and requirements, have set us an example which may, according as we think of them or of ourselves, fill us either with admiration or with shame. Without aid from us they have manfully faced the trouble and the outlay which are the insurance premium that nations must pay for safety from hostile aggression. In Victoria and New South Wales, a navy has been created, first-class works built, armaments of the newest type mounted; while in Australia generally a total sum, I believe, of not less than £5,000,000 has been spent upon defence. In a few weeks from this time, I hope to see with my own eyes the result of these wise and patriotic exertions, and now, on the eve of leaving England for some months, I cannot refrain from again urging

1887. alike upon the Government and the country the vast importance of this question and the deep unwisdom of delay.

I remain, Sir,

Your obedient Servant,

CARNARVON.

HIGHCLERE CASTLE, *August 24th*, 1887.

VIII.

The Earl of Carnarvon said :—

Sir James MacBain, your Excellency,† and
Gentlemen—Very hard indeed do I find it
to express, in adequate terms, my feeling of
gratitude for the honour you have done me,
Sir, in inviting me to this great banquet, and
at the same time to express my acknow-
ledgment to all those gentlemen who have
paid me so great a compliment in being your
guests. Sir, I hardly know how to find words
—I only know this, that the praise you have

* The " Argus," Melbourne, November 26th, 1887.
Dinner in honour of Lord Carnarvon, given on November
25th, 1887, by the President of the Legislative Council
(Sir James MacBain) in the Queen's Hall, Parliament
Houses.

† Sir Henry Loch.

1887. been pleased to bestow upon me, and the
kindly words of his Excellency, far, far tran-
scend any feeble efforts and any poor services
of mine in past days. Yet, Sir, it has been
from first to last my privilege and my honour,
so far as my public life is concerned, to have
been mainly, if not entirely, connected with the
colonial administration of this great Empire.
I began official life in the Colonial Office.
Three times—first as Under Secretary, then
as Secretary of State—I had the honour
of being connected with the Colonial Empire
of England. And, perhaps without vanity, I
may so far say that I constitute in a humble
degree a link between Downing Street and
Young Australia.

Sir, when I first knew the Colonial Office in
my early days, Australia had relations almost
exclusively with England, and those relations
were at once social, commercial, and political. With Europe she had practically no
relations. During the interval on which I

now look back Australia has stepped into 1887. a new position, and has been brought into relationship with Europe. She — whether, gentlemen, you say it is for good or whether you say it is for evil—is taking her place amongst the family of European nations. If Europe is prosperous, then Australia receives some reflex of that prosperity. If thunderstorms growl in the European atmosphere they are heard, and in some degree felt here. In meteorological phraseology the circle of political disturbance is greatly enlarged. It would not be difficult, Sir, to point out to such an audience as this the numberless forms and ways in which Australia and Europe now act and re-act on each other. It is not merely social intercourse—the rapid passage to and fro; it is not merely the bonds of commerce, of credit, in the great European markets; it is not merely, if I may venture to say so, that your own great wealth and prosperity make you an object of interest and

I.D.   G

1887. admiration, and also an object of envy. It is not merely this, but that the mastery of that broad ocean on which a generation ago only a few hardy navigators ploughed their way has now become an object of ambition, as necessary to the acquisition of territory by foreign nations.

Sir, I know how delicate the ground is on which I venture to touch—how many burning questions are conjured up; and yet it would be cowardly if I did not in some way allude to them when they touch the interests of this country so closely. I might call up many examples and illustrations. I will venture on two or three, in order to illustrate what difficulties there often are, and what serious consequences those difficulties may lead to. Sir, you have near here a group of islands well known under the name of New Hebrides. I have seen recently telegraphic communications in the papers of which I do not pretend to know the precise value, but the

history of the New Hebrides serves my pur- 1887.
pose for an illustration, as well as anything
else can. France desires a territory. She
hoists her flag on these islands. We protest
against that assumption of sovereignty. She
enters into an engagement, and she promises
to withdraw that occupation. But as time
goes on France finds that in the diplomacy
of Europe the New Hebrides are a valuable
counter, and she retains them. Then arises,
perhaps, such a complication as that which
has recently arisen in Egypt. French ambition for generations past has been centred in
Egypt, and France negotiates for Egypt with
the New Hebrides in her hand. And finally,
let us suppose, if we are not deceived, the
Egyptian difficulty is solved in favour of
France by her retiring from the New Hebrides.
The New Hebrides is the price for Egypt.
Well, gentlemen, let me say in all frankness,
locally viewed, this is to the clear advantage
of Australia. Imperially viewed, it is for you

1887. to consider whether it does not carry with
it some corresponding more than equivalent
disadvantage ; because the possession of
Egypt and of the Suez Canal is, I hold,
almost as important to you as members of
the British Empire on the banks of the
Yarra as it is to us in London on the banks
of the Thames.

May I venture upon another illustration ?
There is another island, belonging to the
Society Group, by name Raiatea.   Since, I
think, the year 1847 or 1848, about the
period of the Tahiti difficulty, a convention
has existed with France which debarred both
England and France from any possession or
occupation of that island.   Some few years
ago the French flag was hoisted there.   We
have protested repeatedly, and yet France
remains.   Well, I can only say on this, that
either it is our business to endeavour to induce
France to adhere to her engagements or, at
all events, to secure for this country a full

and ample equivalent. One thing only I will say in connection with all these questions— whether the island be large or small, whether the possession be important or unimportant— I trust that all ample means will be found henceforth for safeguarding both Australasian and English commerce. And I have few practical objects in politics more near to my heart at this moment than to see the great stations abroad, where the Queen's Navy must be refitted, where it must be coaled, where it must receive from time to time protection, placed in a position of complete and adequate defence.

Sir, might I venture on yet another illus- tration? There is another island, and not so very far from these shores, where France has thought it right to export a criminal popula- tion. She has converted that fair island into a penal settlement. Now, I have often and often again in England expressed my view of that matter with absolute freedom, and

1887. I know not why in the city of Melbourne
I should practise greater reticence. And
therefore, I will say this, that I hold, and
have always held, that France thereby com-
mitted a great moral wrong against Australia;
that it is against the comity of nations that
any country should keep a band of wild
beasts within its own territory ready to be
discharged upon the shores of a peaceful and
unoffending community. "Ah, but," say my
French friends, "we keep them under bolt
and bar." I say "No, they constantly escape;
and even if they don't, what right have you
to rear up from these twice-polluted, thrice-
contaminated convicts, a brood worse even
than their fathers?" And again, the French
Minister says, "New Caledonia belongs to us,
and this is strictly within our rights." I say,
and I appeal fearlessly to every great lawyer,
there is a law and there is an equity, and by
that equity this brood of criminals is bound
to be restrained. *Sic utere tuo ut alienum non*

lædas, as a maxim of law, is good all the world 1887.
over; and therefore I say, whilst the Imperial
Government cannot be asked or expected to
turn France out from her possession, yet
the Imperial Government has this duty,
that it is bound to remonstrate, that it is
bound to seize every possible opportunity of
abating a nuisance to this part of the world.

On the other hand, there does devolve—may
I say it without offence?—a certain corresponding duty upon you. Whilst we are bound to
the best of our power to reduce such a nuisance
and to safeguard your interests, on the other
hand, let us count upon your patience, your
support, your forbearance, very often in difficult
matters. In dealing with great nations we cannot always invoke the mere engines of force.
Diplomacy is the sole treatment. European
diplomacy, as you well know, is a very complex matter; and therefore all these questions
must be treated, whether for better or worse,
very often slowly, but still they must be treated

1887. diplomatically. But I am confident of this, that if an English Government is known here to have your interests at heart, to be fairly and fully working in that cause, you will never be unreasonable in any of your demands. In other words, the meaning of this is, as I said before, that you are stepping from the position in which local duties, however important, have been your main occupation, into a position wherein Imperial duties and partnership in Imperial labours and dangers will be henceforward your lot.

I know not whether to congratulate you or not. It is a thorny road. It has been sometimes said, " Happy is that people whose annals are tedious." Your annals have not been tedious in the past, and they certainly will not be tedious in the future. And, as I said before, if England and England's Colonies can go on hand in hand, thoroughly trusting in each other, then I for one am convinced that we may confound our enemies, that we may distance our rivals, and that we may face the future, whatever that unknown future is, with perfect confidence. And, therefore, Sir, it is with indescribable pleasure that since I have been on these shores I have been an eye-witness of all those preparations that you in the time of peace have made for war; and I have rejoiced to see the well-constructed forts, the powerful armaments, the well-trained volunteers, the young fleet that is growing up, and still more, if it were possible, I have rejoiced to see carried that Bill which was the outcome of the recent conference in London, that Bill to which allusion has been made to-night, that Bill which binds these Colonies to the Mother Country in the bonds of a common defence. I read in that Bill the best and first of examples. I read in it matter for pride and pleasure by Englishmen all over the world. I read in it still more a deliberate and satisfactory answer made to those foreign nations who look—I will not say

1887. with unfriendly, but yet I shall not be far
wrong if I say with jealous eyes on the
greatness of Britain. And, Sir, much as I
rejoice at that Bill, perhaps I rejoice still
more at the manner in which that Bill was
passed—party differences, personal dissensions
laid aside, unanimity for the common weal
the one sole, guiding principle. One night
sufficed to carry that Bill through all its con-
ventional stages in the House of Assembly,
one more night sufficed for the Legislative
Council; and to-day you, Sir, whose high
privilege it is to represent Her Gracious
Majesty—you, with all the pomp and cere-
monial of befitting circumstance, with the
thunder of guns, a very appropriate concomi-
tant, gave the Royal sanction to that Bill.
Sir, I congratulate you, as Her Majesty's
representative, upon what you have fitly
termed, I think, that high privilege. I congratulate myself on having been here a witness
of these great things. I congratulate, if I

may venture to do so, the statesmanship of Parliament, of Government, and Opposition alike, who joined in it. I congratulate the patriotism of a united people, and I will go yet one step further, and say that in the name of all those who, thousands of miles away across the seas, still hold dear the honour of the old country, I thank the Parliament, the Government, the authorities, and the people of Victoria for the steps they have taken.

Let me not be mistaken. What we in England desire, and what I believe you in Victoria desire, is peace. As was said of some famous Colonies now many years ago, we desire that every man should sit under his own vine and fig tree, and should reap the honest fruits of legitimate labour. But we know also this, that there is no safe or enduring peace which is bought by undue concessions, and that they who respect themselves most are most respected by others. Sir,

1887. there is trouble in Europe, and England has often to plough her way through a sea of anxiety and perplexity. Yet in the midst of all that she can sympathise with the aspirations of these Colonies, and she feels to them as warmly at heart as if they were situate within her own boundaries. I believe, for my own part, that the sun of British enterprise and courage has not gone down. I believe that the mission of Great Britain is not yet fulfilled, perhaps is not yet half fulfilled; but this I do know, that by God's help we will never consent to efface ourselves either here in these southern waters, or in the courts of the councils of Europe.

IX.

MY own opinion on the subject is very generally known. I regard the Colonial Defence
Act as a very useful and valuable measure
indeed, from many points of view. First, it
was a step in the direction of that co-operation
which I have always very strongly contended
for, and which I have endeavoured to promote,
not only when I was in office, but as chairman
of the Defence Commission which sat for many
years. Next, I think the general provisions of
the Bill are effective and satisfactory. Again,
I consider it no objection to say that those
provisions may hereafter require and receive
modification; for that is a feature of all

* The "Brisbane Courier," January 7th, 1888. Interview
at Government House, January 6th, 1888.

1888. such legislation, and particularly legislation on points upon which the relations of the Mother Country and the Colonies are themselves from year to year in process of modification. Further, I believe it to be a measure which is not only desirable but quite necessary in the interests of the Empire, and most of all in the interests of the Australian Colonies. But though not so absolutely essential to Great Britain, it is very valuable to her that she should be seen by foreign nations to have the unhesitating and full support of her Colonies so far as their circumstances allow them to give it. And lastly, I think, looking at it from the colonial point of view, that it is an excellent bargain for the Colonies.

All those different reasons may, of course, be expanded, and are open to a great deal of argument. They admit of support and confirmation on innumerable grounds and by innumerable facts; but the great point which I think it is desirable that we should at this

juncture apprehend is this. In the present 1888.
state of the world there is and can be no
isolated and separate existence for this or for
any other Colony. The varied influences of
peace and of commerce all tend to draw Australia into close union with the older world in
Europe. It is not the connexion with Great
Britain which specially does this, but it is the
rapid intercourse, the regular communication,
and above all the interchange of commerce—
in other words, there cannot now be any of
that separate life which five-and-twenty years
ago was possible; and therefore, whether connected or unconnected with the fortunes of
England, Australia must feel all the influences
of peace and of war which exist in the Old
World. As a consequence of that, the idea
of neutrality in the midst of a great war is an
amiable delusion. None of the great nations
and governments which deal with millions of
men and enormous armaments by land and
sea would for an instant tolerate the neutrality

1888. of a weak State. Although such a Colony as Queensland possesses a vast territory in the present, and will possess a still richer one in the future, if measured by the resources it contains, it is occupied at this moment by a mere handful of people, who would be absolutely powerless in the presence of great national combinations and of the great military and naval agencies with which they would have to deal. On the other hand, it is in the connexion with Great Britain that their real chance of continued safety and prosperity lies—a prosperity and safety that no other State in the world, in my honest opinion, could give them.

I sometimes see the precedent of the United States invoked on the opposite side in this matter; but if any one gives himself the trouble to think for one moment he will see that the illustration is really worthless. When the thirteen Colonies just a century ago separated from Great Britain, their population, it is true, did not, I think, much exceed 3,000,000, which is nearly the present population of Australia; 1883. but in the then state of the world communication was so slow, and intercourse so irregular, and their contact with foreign nations, after our conquest of Canada from the French, so exceedingly small, that the American Colonies were allowed by mere force of circumstances to live and to grow on without check or interference from any great Power. But that is the absolute reverse of the condition of things that now exists in regard to the Australian Colonies; and now that the population of the United States considerably exceeds 40,000,000—I am not sure it is not 50,000,000 —there is not of course the faintest shadow of analogy between their case and that of an Australian Colony.

You tell me that it was in fact argued in Parliament that the advantages accruing from the Imperial connexion would be overshadowed by the disadvantages also accruing. My answer to that, is twofold. First, as I have

1888 already stated, it is not a matter of option
even for a Colony so large and so rich in
natural resources as this. She cannot stand
alone, and if she has not the protection of
Great Britain she must either be absorbed
by some other Power, or she must find a
protector elsewhere." What I mean is that
Queensland would, standing alone, find herself
unequally matched with the great Powers who
desire to found colonial possessions of their
own, and she would be obliged to have re-
course to some protector; and I very much
doubt if she would be able to find one who
would give her the same amount either of
sympathy, or of moral help, or of armed support, as Great Britain would. The support
that Great Britain can give is enormous. It
is not merely as the representative of some
38,000,000 of people in Europe, but it is as
the head of the greatest confederacy and the
greatest Empire that the world has yet seen,
and as such she speaks with an authority

and exercises an influence all over the world 1888.
that nothing but some overwhelming disaster
can modify.

But you suggest that I am dealing now
more with Queensland, by herself, than with
a united Australia, with her own navy, and
that is so. Personally, I should desire to see
the different Australian Colonies drawn much
more closely together. I can see many great
advantages — military and peaceful — which
would flow from such a union, looking at
it from every point of view. But that is in
the future and not a fact of the present; and
even if it were to be accomplished to-morrow
what I have said would only be diminished
pro tanto. Australia, even as a united whole,
with all differences and jealousies cleared
out of the way, would still be unequal
to such a task as that which is sometimes
proposed by a few enthusiasts here. It would
be impossible—it must be seen it would be
impossible for them, without an expenditure

1888. of money that would be simply appalling—
to build, and man, and maintain a fleet that
would be commensurate either with the protection of their great towns or of their coasting
trade, or lastly, of their growing commercial
interests with other parts of the world. The
matter is so clear on this head that it really
does not admit any discussion.

I have watched the proceedings of the
Federal Council of Australasia with some
degree of interest. I must say I never myself
anticipated any extraordinary results from the
present scheme, but I have recognised it as a
useful step in a useful direction. As such I
was glad to see the measure passed into law,
and I think it may be of much advantage
even as it now stands. I sincerely wish the
Council well, and I cannot doubt that, with
the experienced and eminent men that are
upon it, a very good commencement will be
made. And I think I must just add this:
I have always been, as is well known, in

favour of Imperial union, but at the same
time I have never desired to hurry the
matter. I have felt it more prudent to allow
things to grow and to find in circumstances
their own development, though I would also
encourage it and foster it as much as possible. I can see that a very great move has
taken place on the subject lately, and I
am satisfied that public opinion in Australia
generally is much more ripe for further
advances than it was a few years ago. It is
impossible for me to mistake the signs of the
times in that respect ; and I have always
thought and believed that one of the first and
best steps incidental to the creation of a com-
pleter union is a system of common defence.
From that point of view also I therefore look
upon the Naval Defence Bill as a very good
one, and while I desire to express no opinion
on the course which individuals or parties have
pursued here, I must frankly say that I do
regret the loss of the Bill in this Colony.

1888. Not that I think that the enactment of the measure is in any way imperilled. I have very little doubt that it will be passed by your Legislature, and that before long; but I could have wished that the general con-sensus of opinion and action of the Australian Colonies could have been now absolutely complete, and that there had been no exception. Though it is only one exception, and that, as I believe, only temporary, one which really does not impair the proceedings, it does do this: it destroys that appearance of complete unanimity which I especially desire, not so much as regards Australia, not so much as regards England, but as regards the public opinion of Europe. To that extent, and it is not a very large extent, I regret that anything has been allowed to interfere with the appear-ance of the desire of the entire Empire to close up our ranks, and to show an absolutely unbroken front in the face of Europe at a time of unquestionable crisis.

X.

VIEWS ON AUSTRALIAN DEFENCE

Expressed by Lord Carnarvon at an interview in
Adelaide, February, 1888.*

I SHOULD be wrong if I hesitated to express
the opinion that from almost every point of
view at this moment the defence question is
a paramount and pressing one. In some cases
I have, so far as a non-professional person can
speak with any assurance, been satisfied with
the preparations which have been made and
are still in process of making in Australia.
They compare favourably in my mind with
anything that has been done in any other
part of Her Majesty's colonial possessions,
and I will even go further, and say with the
position of things in many parts of the
United Kingdom. I am equally bound in

* The "South Australian Register," February 11th, 1888.

1888. truth to say that there are other places in respect of which much greater exertion is needed. I do not think that it would take very long, or mean a very large expenditure, to ensure a reasonably adequate defence; but I am satisfied that no time ought to be lost, and that every shilling that is judiciously expended is money laid out to the greatest possible advantage.

It is impossible to overrate—whatever may be the final issue—the gravity of the present juncture in Europe; and when you consider what an enormous stake in respect of capital and of present and future prosperity there is in the great towns of these Colonies it seems almost insane, for the sake of a small outlay, to imperil it. I don't think it is possible, from an Australian point of view, to overrate the importance of this.

The recent Naval Defence Bill has added greatly to your security, both in the material force which it will ensure on your coasts for the protection of the towns and the coastal trade, and also quite as much in that it has exhibited to Europe the absolute union of these colonies with the Mother Country for the joint protection of Imperial interests. By Imperial I mean, of course, Australian and British combined.

More, however, remains to be done; and the question of defence is one which will need perpetual vigilance, and, from time to time, adaptation to changing circumstances. On the Home Government lies the burden of placing the coaling stations of the great military outposts in a state of defence; but the time, I hope, will come when, in this part of the world at least, we shall see our way to making one part of the Empire support or assist in the support of the other by a system of well-considered military combination.

I know that in some places there is the idea that in the event of a great war these Colonies might stand aloof from the struggle

1888. under the plea of neutrality. I cannot believe myself that such a course would be possible. The forces engaged, the stake at issue, the prizes that might be won, would be far too large to admit of such a possibility. In the union of the Empire lies its real strength, and, I will also add, its best chances of peace.

When you ask me whether I think that expenditure on defences tends to provoke attack, I reply that I have no belief whatever in that theory. An enemy will attack or abstain from attacking only as may be suggested by the most enlightened and scientific judgment of what is for his interests in a military or naval point of view. All modern warfare shows this. War is decided now simply by scientific and not by moral considerations.

What, of course, I desire very earnestly is to see a greater combination amongst these great Colonies for the purpose of defence. I am quite satisfied that the inclination is there, and I hope that the difficulties which have hitherto stood in the way may before long disappear. I approve of the idea of holding a federal review of the troops. I have always been in favour of some form of combined drill or military practice under canvas, and I have in public more than once said how much importance I attach to this. It is only by these practical experiments that the weak points are ascertained, and the arrangements which would become necessary in a time of actual hostility adequately prepared.

I have a very strong opinion in favour of the proposal to send out one of the leading military experts to inspect Australian defences. The Defence Commission, of which I was chairman, held that it was most important that some such step should be taken. I see myself no difficulty in it. You enquire whom I think best fitted for the work? Well, I know that Lord Wolseley's military reputation stands— and deservedly stands—so high that no name

1888. could be more popular in Australia than his, and there is no one whom I would personally prefer to see execute such a task; but it must always be remembered that his duties at home are very heavy, and that with every desire on his part to meet the wish of Australia he might find it extremely difficult, if not impossible, to be absent from England for so long a period as would be necessary in this case. I can only say that, failing him, I should like to see the next best choice made, and that whenever I have expressed my opinion in public on this point I have always insisted upon the necessity of sending some one whose military reputation and position are such that his opinion would command at once unquestioning assent.

XI.

THE CONDITION OF OUR COALING STATIONS.

Letter to the Editor of the " Times," 9th July, 1888.

SIR,—I have often in your columns called attention to the very unsatisfactory condition of our coaling-stations, and with your permission I now desire in a few words to state what I believe to be substantially the case with regard to the most important of them. I say substantially, because, having no official information, I may perhaps, be wrong in some small details, which, however, will not affect my general conclusions.

These conclusions, I am happy to think, can be more favourably stated now than at any previous time; for at last, after many years of patient, or impatient, expectation, some real progress can be affirmed.

1888.   With one great exception, to be noticed later, the more important stations are being armed.

Singapore is in possession of a part of her new armament, though a large and perhaps the most important portion of it is not yet mounted and available.

Hong Kong is not quite so far advanced, but will soon be similarly provided. Those armaments, however, are, as I have said, numerically still imperfect, and the 10 inch guns, of which so much has been said, are wanting in both places. But, though I will not on such a subject speak with the knowledge of professional authority, I believe that the very serious risks to which we were exposed a short time since are materially diminished.

In Mauritius also the works are proceeding, though I fear that more than a year must elapse before they are complete; and I can only hope that there will be no delay in supplying the new armament, as soon as the forts are ready for its reception. Meanwhile, some guns 1888. of the old muzzle-loading type are available on an emergency.

In St. Lucia—the military value of which, once great, and subsequently reduced, has now revived—both works and armament are making progress, though not so rapid as I could desire.

In Trincomalee and St. Helena, positions to which the Admiralty have always attached much importance, the works are nearly, if not quite, finished; while of Aden, on whose em- battled rock I looked with interest only a few weeks since, a satisfactory record may, I believe, be made.

Of the great Australian Colonies, it would need more than this brief letter to speak adequately. They put us to shame, for with smaller means they have shown an appreciation of the risks of modern war, and of the require- ments of modern defence, which English Gov- ernments have been slow to understand. New Zealand, which enjoys the advantage of a most

1888. able Engineer officer as Governor,* is well armed; Victoria has organised her guns, her forts, her ships, and her forces with a care and completeness which we should do well to follow, and which merit praise higher and fuller than my pen can express; New South Wales has not spared expense in guns of the newest pattern, though they are not yet placed and mounted, and made as available as they should be; South Australia and Queensland are, I believe, in earnest in their preparations; and Tasmania, the least wealthy of this great group of English communities, has forts and guns incomparably better than any to which our commercial ports at home can pretend.

So far, then, we may be reasonably content with the progress now making in our coaling stations; but there are two observations to be made:—

1. That it is only after years of ceaseless speaking, writing and protest that this progress

* Sir William Jervois.

has been made, and that even now there is 1888.
not one of these larger Imperial stations which,
in the strict sense of the word, can be called
complete in its military preparations—complete as Germany, or France, or Italy would
require it to be.

2. That the extremely grave question of
garrisons is, so far as any real action is concerned, untouched, though I presume that in
official phraseology it is, like many other questions, being "considered." But so long as
this subject remains undetermined, the defence
of the stations, and with them the defence of
our vast commerce afloat, are not provided
for. It is useless to build forts at great expense, and to place modern and scientifically
constructed guns in them, unless there are also
properly trained garrisons; and though there
are places which I could name where marines
—that "royal and loyal" corps as they have
been well called—would form the best defence,
this does not apply to all, or to the most

I.D.   I

important of our stations. It is not possible to exaggerate the importance or the urgency of this subject. It doubtless raises some inconvenient considerations, and it means expense; but it must be faced, and, above all, it must be viewed as a whole. It would take too long here to discuss the "how" and the "when," but it is not a question of merely providing fresh troops in all cases. I am confident that in some places a judicious re-arrangement, in others, an employment of local resources, might greatly facilitate the solution of the problem.

I said in the earlier part of this letter that there was one exception to the general progress which I have recorded, and that exception is the Cape, the most important of all our stations, the half-way house between West and East, invaluable for coaling and refitting, for protecting our own commerce, and assailing our enemy's fleets. So strongly did the Commission of which I was chairman hold this

opinion, that they postponed every other con- 1888.
sideration to press upon the then Government
the vital necessity of placing the Cape in an
adequate state of defence; and no one has
ventured to deny or question our recommendations. But years have passed, and Governments have come and gone, and for the
purposes of modern war the Cape is still
undefended. It is right to say that the works
are now in actual process of construction, and
that a much better condition of affairs may
be expected; but I do not believe that as yet
there is a single modern gun mounted in a
single modern fort. When I was at the Cape
eight months ago, there were new forts without their proper armament, and new armaments
expected for forts which had as yet no existence
—an unfortunate, but a not very uncommon
illustration of our procedure in these matters.
I much doubt whether even now there are
any new guns at the Cape.

I have thought that at this moment it may

1888. not be without interest and value to state the actual position of our coaling stations; and I have endeavoured to state it as impartially and correctly as I can. It is a picture of lights and shadows—of progress made, of needless and unfortunate delays, and, lastly, of much important work yet to be done. I might easily add to it the consideration of many other questions of the highest importance connected with the subject; but I prefer to confine myself to those on which I have written; and I have the honour to remain, Sir,

Your obedient Servant,

CARNARVON.

43, PORTMAN SQUARE, *July 5th*, 1888.

XII.

THE CONDITION OF OUR COALING STATIONS.

Letter to the Editor of the " Times," 19th
February, 1889.

SIR,—On the eve of another Session of
Parliament I will once more ask you to allow
me to say a few words upon the present condition of our foreign coaling stations.

When last I wrote on this subject I indulged
the hope that, by the beginning of this year,
the most important of these stations would be
practically secure from hostile attack; but
this anticipation, I am sorry to say, has not
been fulfilled. Let me take the whole chain
of Imperial stations from Plymouth to China,
on which the security of our vast trade in time
of war confessedly depends; and I shall not
be in excess of the facts if I say that not one
is in a state of adequate defence.

1889.   Of Gibraltar, which has been, I fear, a sink of ill-considered expenditure, I will say nothing except that those who know the circumstances know that it is out of accord with the necessities of modern warfare.

Next to Gibraltar in geographical succession comes Sierra Leone. It is a post that was after very careful consideration by the Commission of 1878, of which I was chairman, reported to be strategically of great value, situated as it is halfway between Gibraltar and the Cape, on the track of our Eastern commerce, and within two days' steam of the French settlement of Dakar, where there is always a considerable military force stationed. The advice of the Commission has been so far followed that forts have been constructed; but here all real effort has ceased, and there are neither gunners nor armament. Some obsolete guns alone exist; and in the event of war with France, Sierra Leone would be immediately occupied; the forts which we

have built would, unless recaptured by a costly 1889.
expedition, be destroyed or turned against us,
and our line of communication with the East
would be broken. I do not deny some *primâ
facie* difficulty in finding suitable garrisons for
such a place as Sierra Leone, but it is one
which, by a careful adaptation of means to the
end, could, I know, be overcome; and anyhow
it is obviously worse than idle to construct
forts at these critical points on the great sea-
roads and then to leave them, without armaments and the requisite troops, to the mercy
of our enemies on the outbreak of hostilities.

I could say much more on the subject of
Sierra Leone, for it is an important and a
typical case, but I pass from it to the Cape
—undoubtedly the most important link in the
whole chain of Imperial stations; and here
the same story is to be told. The Commission of 1878 urged, in the strongest terms they
could employ, the immediate defence of the
Cape upon the then Government, as the first

1889. and most urgent work, to which all other considerations should be postponed. The Colonial Government, on the other hand, have shown their readiness to co-operate, but our delays — and, I must add, our irresolution — have been such that, though the forts are built or building, the armament which gives value to the forts is wanting. I am confident that there cannot be more than a single modern heavy gun, if there be one, sent out for the defence of this vital position.

At Mauritius there are only muzzle-loading guns of the old type; at Hong Kong there are some modern guns; and at Singapore, where the local community have faithfully fulfilled their share of the agreement with the Home Government, there are also a few. Whether carriages and mountings are complete I know not, but certainly in neither of these cases is there any armament as heavy as a 9-inch gun. Such delay is neither creditable nor safe; and if it were not a more than jesting

matter your readers might be amused to hear 1889.
that for some weeks last year there appeared in
the "agony column" of one of your contempo-
raries a plaintive inquiry for these guns, which
had been paid for by the Singapore Colony,
which had been promised by the Home Government, but which had somehow and somewhere
gone astray. Thus, exclusive of Gibraltar and
Malta, of which I say nothing, Sierra Leone,
the Cape, Mauritius, Singapore, and Hong
Kong, which should be fully armed, remain
either partially or wholly unprotected; nor
could they be defended in time of war by the
Navy, which would have other duties to perform.

For this very unsatisfactory result I dis-
tinctly say I do not blame the present
Secretary of State for War. If it depended
on him I believe the state of affairs would be
different; the blame must be more widespread,
and unless and until a radical change is made
in our whole administrative system this disas-
trous confusion will continue.

1889.   Where everything is so much amiss it is hardly worth while to single out special errors, but perhaps our chief present deficiency consists in a total inability to obtain the scientific and especially the heavy guns of modern type which we require. Our home fortresses are not supplied, our commercial ports are destitute of them, our Navy is not yet even fully armed, our coaling and Imperial stations abroad are, as I have said, partially or wholly unarmed. The construction, indeed, of forts is a matter of secondary importance; they can be extemporised, and modern science is reverting to primitive practice in preferring earthworks to stone fortifications. But it needs time to build a modern gun, and we are so incompetent or unlucky that either the guns are not produced, or, when forthcoming after long delay, and subjected to trial, they break down, as was the case last year in certain memorable instances.

This, then, is our position. We have fallen

hopelessly into arrear in the international race of armaments; our Governmental establishments cannot produce the required gun; the few manufacturers, like Armstrong and Whitworth, are unable to supply them to the extent and within the time needed; and neither they nor any other English firm will lay down the expensive plant which would enable them to manufacture the required article, unless the Government will give them some assurance of sufficiently large orders to make it worth their while to incur the outlay. There is absolutely no alternative, as far as I can see, but to submit either to the humiliation of purchasing from foreign makers, or to accept the risk of being unarmed when all the nations of the world are armed to the teeth.

I am not asking for impossibilities. What we with our vast resources at home fail to do, the Colony of Victoria has successfully achieved. She has purchased, transported 12,000 miles, and placed in position guns of

1889. the best and most recent pattern; and, if I am not mistaken, she is in possession of some of the newest implements of modern warfare, which our prudence or economy forbids us to acquire.

We are now on the eve of a new Session; the country is anxiously looking to the Government to place both Army and Navy on a more efficient footing, and those of us who have had to bear the reproach of alarmists and panic-makers are now acknowledged to be perfectly right. But it is not enough to spend money; and I trust that the proposals which will be submitted to Parliament will be governed by larger and wiser views than has often been the case. Our past record is one of continual shortcoming. We have carried prudence into timidity, and economy into parsimony; we spend where we should be sparing, we save where we should spend; and we too often postpone a wise decision or defer a necessary reform to obtain something better, which, after all, is never secured. Our principle is 1889. exactly the reverse of that which has guided to victory the German Government, who have adopted as their standard readiness and fitness for war, instead of some ideal perfection which entails years of delay, and ends in ultimate disappointment.

I remain, Sir,

Your obedient Servant,

CARNARVON.

43, PORTMAN SQUARE, *February 15th*, 1889.

XIII.

Discussion at the Royal United Service Institution,
March 1st, 1889.

THE EARL of CARNARVON said :—Sir Frederick
Stephenson and Gentlemen, You are very
good to call upon me to contribute what
little I can say to this most interesting
discussion, though, as a civilian, I naturally
feel great diffidence in addressing an audience
which I know is so largely composed of professional experts and men well calculated to
express a public opinion on such a subject. I
had, however, the advantage, Sir, of being connected for some years with a Commission which
was authorised to inquire into our defences
abroad. It led me to look very closely into
these questions, and I am bound to say that
the opinion that I then formed does not concur

with the views which the gallant Admiral* has set forth with so much ability this evening.

I will not, of course, enter upon what is really the larger half of this question, the defences of our arsenals and our commercial ports in these Islands. I am afraid I must dispose of the one by saying that they are only very partially armed, and of the second that they are absolutely defenceless at present. I would rather, in the few observations which I would make, speak of those foreign stations with which I myself and the very able Commission which acted with me were empowered to deal. I apprehend, putting it in perfectly civilian and untechnical fashion, that the defence of the Empire consists really of two things—the defence of our home shores on the one hand, and the defence of our commerce afloat on the other, for our commerce is our life and being, and if it be destroyed our credit and resources perish with it. I

* Rear-Admiral P. H. Colomb.

fully subscribe to the doctrine which has been laid down here to-night, and elsewhere, that our first line of defence is the Navy; and more than that, I think we have been living in a state of—I hardly like to use the words that were on my lips, but I will say we have lived for some years in a fool's paradise, trading on our past reputation, and utterly deficient in the necessary means of self-protection. With regard to the necessary amount and character of our naval defences, I will only say that the Commission of which I had the honour to be the chairman, having to examine incidentally and collaterally into that subject, came to a distinct and a decided opinion on the subject, and represented to the Government of the day, and consequently to their successors, that in our opinion the naval defences of the Empire were inadequate for the purpose, and I need not say how grave such a statement was.

But I pass to a second branch of this question, the protection of our commerce afloat.

Now, Sir, the view of the Commission was this : that inasmuch as there were great lines of English commerce of incalculable value, to be registered not by hundreds and thousands, but perhaps by millions of pounds, it was of inestimable importance that we should hold the commanding points along those great sea routes. By some strange accident of fortune the principal of those governing points have fallen into the hands of this country, and it seems to me to be almost madness not to take the full advantage of them. And let me observe that when persons talk of the vast expense to which this leads us, I would observe that this is very exaggerated language. The expense of defending these coaling stations is really most moderate ; and, looking to the object which is in view, it bears no kind of proportion to it. The estimate which the Commission made of the expense represents in round numbers not very much more than the cost of two large ships of war

of the present day. I leave it, therefore, to
the common sense of such an audience as this,
whether it is reasonable to shrink from such
an outlay, the absence of which may mean
the loss of the best part of our commerce
afloat.

Now, Sir, what is it that makes these fortified
coaling stations and harbours so valuable? I
apprehend, speaking roughly and generally, that
you might classify their advantages pretty much
under these heads. First, it is intended by
arming these coaling stations that the Queen's
fleet in those distant parts of the world should
be set free to operate as naval policy may
direct. Secondly, after an action our fleets are
enabled under the security of the guns of those
defended stations to refit and to repair. Has
anybody ever considered what the expense, difficulty, impossibility, would be of sending home
from an enormous distance some of our large
men-of-war in order to repair and to refit?
Thirdly, the Queen's ships are enabled not only

to refit and repair, but to coal; and as Sir Lothian Nicholson very truly said, coal under present conditions has become the very life of a ship; she cannot move without it, she is absolutely dependent upon it; and moreover, every one knows well that whereas our first-class commercial ships can carry and do carry a very large amount of coal, the Queen's ships can carry but a very limited quantity. But further, just in the same way these coaling stations afford shelter to our commercial navy, when, chased by privateers or pursued by enemies, they take refuge under the guns of those forts. In the same way, too, they are enabled to coal, and if this protection be not given to them, it is almost certain that either two thirds of the commercial marine must be laid up on the outbreak of war, inasmuch as the vessels would not be adequate in point of speed to escape the fast cruisers of our enemies, or that on the other hand, we should see two thirds of them transferred to a foreign flag. It must be borne in mind that in all probability the days of convoying a merchant fleet are passed. Lastly, we must not forget that defended stations have the tendency at all events greatly to deter an enemy's cruisers. A foreign ship of war will, I apprehend, think twice and thrice before she attempts to force a reasonably armed defended station. She would run the risk of injury to herself, the certain risk of a vast expenditure of her coal, and lastly, the risk of an expenditure of her ammunition, and all this at a distance from her own base. On all these grounds, the Commission with which I was connected thought that the effective arming of these coaling stations offered very great advantages both to the Queen's Navy and also to our commercial marine.

But I must take the liberty of saying this, that if these forts are not to be reasonably equipped and defended it would be better that we should not touch them at all. On that I entertain a very clear opinion. You need for these positions not merely forts, but you need the guns to put into these forts, and you need trained gunners and garrisons to defend them; and if you are not prepared to go to that amount of preparation it is better that you should not waste time and money upon a fruitless and perhaps mischievous object. And yet, as a matter of fact, that, I am afraid, is really the present position of things. We have a considerable number of these stations on which great expense has been incurred, sometimes by ourselves, sometimes by our inducing the Colonial and local authorities to undertake the work; we have fortifications erected at a large outlay, but in the vast majority of cases we have either only guns of a very small calibre, or no guns at all; and in one case I have repeatedly protested—I have exhausted myself in protesting—against the policy, I should say the insanity, of leaving such a vital point as the Cape of Good Hope for years and years undefended.

When our Commission, to which I have already alluded, was appointed in 1879, the first subject that came before us was the defence of the Cape. We went into the question knowing its vast importance as an imperial station, we postponed everything else to press this one question upon the consideration of the Government. We did so press it: we reported immediately and fully on it; and I can truly say that I myself have never lost an opportunity whether in public or in private, of urging it upon successive Governments; and yet at this moment, though the forts are built or building, there is practically no armament whatever in them. I do not say there is special blame to any particular Government. The blame must be widespread. The country is to blame by its apathy and indifference to dangers which, because they are not immediately visible, are disregarded; but now that the question has come before the country, I hold it to be the bounden duty of all those who can by voice or vote bring pressure to bear, to use that influence to the uttermost for the common good.

And now may I, in conclusion, say this, that whilst admiring the ability with which the paper which the gallant Admiral has read to-day has been drawn up, I cannot subscribe to it. I think that the gallant Admiral has attempted to prove too much. I fully admit with him that the Navy is the first line. I wish to see that Navy strengthened, and I trust to see that this new Session of Parliament will not pass without a very considerable increase; but, on the other hand, if our coaling stations and ports, both at home and abroad, are not to be placed in a state of defence, then I hold that the gallant Admiral has asked us to go into, not a large, but an enormous, an overwhelming expenditure for naval purposes. The absence of defended ports means a naval increase to which it seems to me difficult to set any limit. I think we are in danger at the present moment of what I may call a see-saw of opinion. We have on the one side a very able body of men who represent to us, as I believe most truly, that the Navy requires a large increase. Probably there may be a tendency to carry that view a little too far, but on this I do not now argue. On the other hand, we have a body of able men who warn us of the risk of invasion, and who actually desire to surround this vast metropolis with fortifications. Sir, as a mere civilian who by your favour this afternoon am allowed to address a professional audience, I must honestly say that I believe the truth lies somewhere in a mean between the two conflicting views. I believe there is great necessity for the increase of the Navy. I believe also that reasonable defence ought to be given to our coaling stations and home ports, and this without the loss of an hour. I hope and believe that we shall see a real and effective step made this year. We shall be probably asked for a considerable sum; but it is not only the expenditure of money that will secure the object that we have in view, the need is that such an expenditure should be governed by large and wise and statesmanlike considerations.

XIV.

Speech in the House of Lords, March 29th, 1889.

THE EARL OF CARNARVON, on rising to inquire whether Her Majesty's Government could give any information as to the time when the Commission appointed last year to consider the administration of the Naval and Military Departments would report; also whether it was part of the duty of the Commission to report whether the great delays in the manufacture and production of guns were due to defects in our administrative system, said :—

Your lordships will doubtless remember the general object of this Commission, and the circumstances under which it was appointed

last year. The Commission is a very important one. Lord Hartington is the chairman ;
the First Lord of the Treasury and Lord
Randolph Churchill are among its members.
It was much debated at the time of the
appointment of the Commission whether some
means should not be provided for fixing
authoritatively the standard of military and
naval strength. I think myself that no one
will really be satisfied until this is somehow
defined. If such a standard could be fixed,
a great deal of present controversy would be
saved, and we should no longer, as now, be
working very often in the dark. But that
was not the decision which was then arrived
at, and Her Majesty's Government recommended the appointment of a Commission,
which was "to consider the administration
of the Military and Naval Departments"—
in fact, to consider what should be the relations between those departments and between
each of them and the Treasury.

1889. My lords, this is not by any means the
first Commission on this subject that has been
appointed. Some of your lordships may have
read, and if you have you will have read with
very great interest and admiration, the report
of the Commission appointed about two years
ago, of which the learned Judge, Sir Fitzjames
Stephen, was chairman, on the system under
which the patterns of warlike stores are made
and passed into Her Majesty's Service. That
report, to which I must refer, is not only
characterised by great ability, but contains
statements of the most serious nature. To
that Commission was referred the question of
corruption in certain cases. The Commissioners acquitted those who were charged with
corruption, but they certainly pronounced an
extremely heavy censure upon the Administrative Departments upon the ground of
inefficiency. They went so far indeed as to
imply, if not to say in so many words, that it
is almost, in present circumstances, a chaotic

system. They dwelt very much on the im- portance of decentralisation, and I think everyone who has turned his attention to the subject will be prepared to admit that in that they were eminently right. But if I understand rightly the present position of affairs in the War Office, recent changes have been rather in the opposite direction. My right hon. friend, the Secretary of State for War, *in a speech made a short time since, expressed his intention of decentralising in certain cases. My right hon. friend has my hearty good wishes in that object, though I could desire that the decentralising process were carried a good deal farther than is apparently contemplated.

I would ask your lordships to consider for one moment what the position of the Secretary of State for War really is. He has to discharge a number of functions and duties which, physically and mentally, are absolutely beyond the scope of any living man. There are no less

* The Hon. Edward Stanhope.

1889. than five different capacities in which he acts. First of all, he has duties as a Cabinet Minister, which involve the careful consideration of the most varied and important matters; secondly, he has to deal with questions in Parliament of a military character; thirdly, the whole of the Stores and the Ordnance pass under his review; fourthly, the enormous question of Fortifications comes under his charge; and lastly, he is responsible for the Army Estimates in their preparation and passage through Parliament. He is, moreover, in nine cases out of ten, a civilian, who has to learn his business when he goes to the War Office; he is constantly changed, and, therefore, we cannot possibly secure anything like a continuity of military policy. Between 1881 and 1887 there have been no less than six Secretaries of State for War—on the average, one a year. What is the result of all this? It is an entire absence of individual responsibility, running from top to bottom of our system. There

are cutlasses which will not cut, swords that 1889.
break, bayonets that bend, cartridges that jam,
saddlery that is defective, and stores which are
absolutely vicious and bad ; and there are guns
designed and ordered years and years before
they ever come to completion, and when they
do, they are sometimes practically worthless.
What the country complains of is that the
responsibility cannot be fixed on any one
person, or even on one part of the system ;
the consequence being that no individual is
ever punished.

I read with great interest the other day the
statement of the Secretary of State for War.
As to the coaling stations, my right hon.
friend frankly admitted that what I and others
have been complaining of for so long was the
case, and that at this moment, after eight
or nine years of waiting, virtually none of
these stations are in an adequately defensible
condition. My right hon. friend went on to
promise the larger guns, and in this I hope

1889. he was not too optimistic in his calculations. Those large guns are almost the first and most pressing need. They have been promised for a very long time, but at this moment none of the large 9·2-inch type are mounted, at home or abroad. I do not blame any individual; but, speaking generally, this position of affairs is scandalous. For years and years those guns have been promised, and year after year large sums of money have been voted for them; and yet at the end of all this time we are still without that which is considered to be essential. The only way of escape from the difficulty is to hand over the contracts to private firms. We are in terrible arrears. This country cannot be compared in these matters with France, Germany, Italy, the United States, or even with some of our own Colonies, where the best of guns exist, which have been obtained from private manufacturers. I believe from what I have heard that at this moment the

United States has a certain number of the 1889.
9·2-inch guns which we have never been able
to procure.

How far, then, is our administrative system
and organisation responsible for those great
defects? A good many years ago, but not out
of the recollection of many of your lordships,
the Ordnance Department formed a branch
separate from the duties of the Secretary for
War and for the Colonies, these two offices
being then conjoined in one Minister, who
embraced the double functions of War Minister
and Colonial Minister. The Master-General
was at the head of the department. He was
an officer of the highest rank and status; he
was, so to speak, a permanent officer, and in
many instances he sat in the Cabinet of the
day, as in the case, among others, of Lord
Hardinge and the Duke of Wellington. I
have heard from many persons in former years
of the great advantage derived by the Cabinet
from the presence of the Duke of Wellington

1889. in the consideration of all military questions. I think that was a wise plan, so far as it went; but at the time of the Crimean War, when our military arrangements were re-organised in great haste, and in circumstances of much confusion, most of the duties of the Ordnance Department were transferred to the Secretary of State for War. In 1863 the Secretary at War was abolished, and then, again, about 1869 the Surveyor-General's Department was created, the object being to have at the head of the department to which was transferred the business of the Ordnance, not only a military officer, but also, if possible, a member of the House of Commons. But very soon the professional element dropped out, and a civilian was appointed. Since then, I believe that the great majority of Surveyors-General have been civilians; and not only are they engaged in political life and continually changed, but they are under the influence of their so-called subordinates in the War Office.

Here, again, is another instance of the want 1889. of responsibility on which I lay so much stress. Eight or nine years ago the Ordnance Committee was established. It was a body partly composed of civilians and partly of officers; but inasmuch as it changes periodically, it is impossible to fix responsibility upon it. The chain of responsibility extends from the Secretary of State, through the Commander-in-Chief, the Director of the Ordnance Committee, the subordinate officers who have to deal with the branches of the business, down to the manufacturer. It is absolutely impossible, when a gun bursts, to fix the responsibility on any one of the different persons or departments which I have enumerated. This means a very serious state of affairs, and yet it exists in nearly every branch of the Service. I will trouble your lordships with but a single quotation, and that is very apt. In the Egyptian campaign it was stated in the evidence before the Commission that—

1889. "Out of 110 shrapnell shell, 55 were found defective, some having no bursting charges, and others having the bursting charges wet. Out of a total of 398 shrapnell shells, 156 were found correct—that is, about 39 per cent; 125 portion of bursting-charge gone—about 31 per cent.; 61 empty—about 16 per cent.; 30 damp—about 8 per cent.; and 26 jammed—about 7 per cent."

The comment of Lord Wolseley upon that statement is as follows:—

"*April* 13*th*, 1885.

"My Lord,—It is difficult for me to adequately describe the feelings with which I have read the inclosed papers describing the condition of the ammunition supplied from Woolwich to the only battery of Royal Artillery which accompanied the column recently operating from Korti across the Bayuda Desert. In all our small wars the British soldier has to contend against enemies vastly superior in

number, and it is only by superior discipline 1889.
and the efficiency of our arms of precision
that we can secure victory. I have already
addressed your lordship on the subject of the
carelessness shown by those responsible at
home for the quality of the ammunition supplied to the troops in the field, in issuing star
shells of a different calibre from that of the
guns of the battery serving here. I trust the
new proof contained in the inclosed papers of
the culpable negligence of some branch of the
department at home will lead to an inquiry into
its working by a board of selected officers of
the line, unconnected in every way with the
Woolwich manufacturing or store department,
or with the administration under which they
work. I write strongly because I feel strongly
when I think of how the lives of gallant sol-
diers may have been sacrificed in the present
campaign, and may be again so sacrificed in
the future, through the inexcusable carelessness
of individuals in the Woolwich Arsenal, and

1889. through the unsoundness of a system under which such ammunition as that described in these inclosures could possibly have been issued for service in the field.

" I have, &c.,

" WOLSELEY (General)."

It is needless to comment upon that. Indeed, I should only weaken such a letter by doing so. Sir Fitzjames Stephen's report summed up the opinion of the Commissioners as to the present defects in this particular weapon. They said that our system had no definite object, and no efficient head; and, lastly, no definite practical method of dealing with all those technical and scientific stores and implements which had to be dealt with. It is impossible to conceive a stronger or a more sweeping statement than that, and yet, as a matter of fact, I have never heard it contradicted or controverted in any way. If the state of things be as described, of course we are convicted of very great waste and ineffi- ciency. Efficiency and economy generally go hand in hand, but our system is against both. No doubt, under our Parliamentary system we cannot have the vigour and the rapidity of action and the mobility of foreign Governments. But, on the other hand, there are also great difficulties arising out of our management of that system, and the organisation which we have created. For this we are responsible, and on these questions I hope the Commission will be able to make full and adequate recommendations. The Commissioners are so constituted that they ought to do so; but, on the other hand, we must always look in the main and in the end to Her Majesty's Government. They have, of course, the spending of this large sum of £18,000,000 a year. They have the real power and the real responsibility. I do not doubt their wish to do what is right, and I have not made these observations with the

1889. object of casting blame on any individual. It is because I am impressed with the serious position of circumstances that I desire to call attention to some at least of the most important factors in this case, and to point out how great, in my opinion, is the evil, how great is the waste, how great is the danger, and how great is the need of finding a remedy with the least possible delay.

XV.

Address to the London Chamber of Commerce,
December 10th, 1889.

I NEED not, to such an audience as this,
dwell on the importance of our trade with the
Australasian Colonies, or its money value, or
on the constant growth of the communications, by steamer, by post, by telegraph, which
every year seem to knit us more closely in
sympathy, as well as in interest, with our kinsfolk across the seas. For present purposes it
is sufficient to say that the trade flows in
three large streams between Great Britain
and those Colonies—through the Suez Canal,
by the Cape, and round Cape Horn. By
the Suez route it represented in 1887 some
£24,000,000, by the Cape route £13,000,000,

1889. and by the Horn £9,000,000—a vast amount
of property to be afloat between these two
branches of the British race, and worthy of
every reasonable care and safeguarding on both
sides of the globe.   Large as the figures are,
I believe they may hereafter become much
larger ; but whether that be so or not, whether,
indeed, they remain such as they are, depends
on the manliness and sagacity of Australia
and England.

Besides this enormous trade, we cannot
forget the immense wealth which is centred in
at least the two great cities of Sydney and
Melbourne, and further, how large a part of
that wealth represents English capital; nor,
again, how large a part of that wealth and
capital is based upon the complicated and
delicate element which we call credit, and
which is preserved in its integrity by the
sense of security from any hostile attack;
nor, lastly, need I speak of the intimate con-
junction of political, commercial, and personal

interests in which England and Australia are bound up. In the forcible words of an Australian statesman, whose acquaintance I have had the pleasure of making, " We cannot imagine any description of circum- stances by which the Colonies should be weakened or humiliated or lowered, under which the Empire itself would not be itself weakened, humiliated, or lowered. And we are unable to conceive any circumstances under which the wealth and status of the Colonies could be increased, which would not increase in the same degree the wealth and status of the Empire." The question therefore which I desire to bring before you to-day—though it must necessarily be rapidly and in outline—is how these vast and widely ramified interests are to be protected in a time of war, and in what proportions by the two Partners, as I may not unfitly call them, in our Imperial Firm.

What, then, is the relative position of the

1889. two parties, and what do they severally contribute to the common object? On the one
side, this country provides the whole fleet—
that which is stationed in Australian waters,
that which is in reserve, that which is in support in other parts of the world—because, for
efficient common defence these elements, the
men, the guns and material, and the knowledge and directing head, must be united under
one control. She provides also the great coaling stations, with their armaments and garrisons, which, rightly organised, enable the
Royal Navy to keep the seas and ensure so
largely the protection of Australian commerce;
such as the Cape, Ceylon, Singapore, Hong
Kong; and, lastly, she furnishes those swift
mail steamers and merchantmen, armed or
unarmed, "the greyhounds of the ocean" as
they have been termed, which, whether as
irregular cruisers or as carriers of merchandise
and supplies, must play so large a part in any
future war.

On the other side, the Australian Colonies 1889. contribute, under the recent agreement, a certain money subsidy towards the maintenance of the local fleet. They provide the landworks and armaments which defend their own coasts and shipping, as well as the ships of the British Navy, when for any reason they may need to retire to refit or repair in Australian ports; they provide in a few cases some ships and gunboats for harbour defence ; they furnish a small, well-paid, and trained permanent force, together with a considerable body of volunteers, which, though very satisfactory in character and spirit, yet needs in many important respects further organisation. This, very briefly stated, is, I think, a fair statement of what Great Britain and Australasia are supposed to contribute towards the common object of defence in Australasian waters.

Any one who will compare this state of things with that of a few years since will see how considerable has been the advance made.

1889. In 1879, just ten years ago, Sir William Jervois based his plan of defence on the principle that whilst the Imperial Navy undertakes the protection of British trade afloat, the Australian Colonies should at their own cost provide the local forces, forts, and other appliances for the protection of their principal ports. Again, at the Intercolonial Conference, held at Sydney in 1881, a resolution was agreed to that the naval defence of these Colonies should remain the exclusive charge of the Imperial Government, that the squadron should be strengthened, and that the several Colonies should at their own cost place the land defence on an effective footing. Lastly, a year after this, in 1882, the Commission for the Defence of British Possessions Abroad, of which I had the honour to be chairman, though acknowledging the expediency of the money contribution, which has now been adopted, hesitated, and wisely hesitated in the then state of Colonial feeling, to press it on the Colonies.

It will thus be seen how large a step has been 1889. taken since 1879, 1881, and 1882 by the agreement entered into by this country and the Australian Colonies in 1887.

But since then another, and in my opinion an important move has been made along the same road. The Defence Commission, of which I have spoken, strongly recommended the appointment of an experienced officer of rank and distinction to inspect the forces and military establishments of the Australian Colonies, and this recommendation has been at last complied with. General Bevan Edwards has inspected the defences of the great Australian Colonies, and is now, I believe, visiting, or about to visit, New Zealand. His report promises to bear abundant fruit. I do not know what precisely his recommendations are; but I cannot doubt that in any proposals for the general defence of Australia, they would, among many others, contain these—the enactment of measures to enable in time of war or in certain

1889. specified circumstances the forces of one Colony to cross the borders of another, and a General Discipline Act for the control of joint Colonial forces, and for placing them under a single authority. It is hardly less necessary to establish a manufactory of gunpowder, small arms ammunition, and the minor kinds of warlike stores; but until the arrangements for this have been matured, a depôt of these supplies might easily be formed. It is a matter of importance; for on the outbreak of hostilities the strain upon our resources at home would be such that it would be impossible to send munitions of war abroad to the Colonies in adequate quantities.

It is doubtful whether matters are ripe in Australia for the establishment of a school of military instruction such as exists at Kingston in Canada. I look back always with the greatest satisfaction upon the share which I had in the creation of that school, and when I was in Canada some years since, I saw with unfeigned delight the satisfactory condition

in which it then was; but neither the pre- 1889.
sent circumstances nor the feeling in Australia
make such a school necessary—and it must
wait.

These are some of the changes which are
necessary to enable the Australian Colonies to
perform their part in the common work and
duty to which I have referred. Most, if not
all of them would be best accomplished
through the agency of a Common Federal
Legislature, if such existed; but it is possible
that the end may be achieved, though less
perfectly, by the existing machinery. Whatever may be the means adopted, I think they
are all of pressing importance.

Having thus stated the position of the two
parties, it remains to consider what should
be the principles and the proportions of the
co-operation at which we aim. Taking the
British side first, it is clear that in war-time
the main duties must fall on the Navy; though
till we are actually engaged in hostilities

1889 it is impossible to say precisely what those
duties will be. The wisest heads amongst us
cannot venture to predict what a maritime
war will be, and will involve; there have been
many great wars on land during the last thirty-
five years, but we have had comparatively
no precedents or experience of naval warfare
within that time. Much at the best is con-
jecture. But we know this much—that it
must rest with this country to find the ships
and the crews, to maintain and if necessary
to increase the Australian squadron, to keep
the lines of communication open both as regards commerce and supplies; to fight any
enemies that may show themselves, to silence
and clear out any military stations that they
may possess or acquire in those seas; to catch
any piratical or privateering ships of the
Alabama class, and finally to keep up in full
efficiency those fortified coaling stations on
which the fighting power of the Navy and the
safety of our merchantmen depend. Truly a

long and weighty list of duties, but of which 1889. not one can be omitted without the risk of entire failure.

And here, in passing, I will venture to pay a tribute, even at our own expense, to the good sense of the Australian negotiators who were parties to the Agreement of 1887. The Defence Commission, of which I was chairman, had laid it down strongly that, in the event of any subsidy from the Colonies, the Australian squadron should not be tied in its operations to any particular spot, and that the officer in command should be free to handle his ships not only how, but where he pleased. But at the time of the negotiation of the agreement, our authorities, in their desire to conciliate what they supposed to be the objections of the Colonists, seemed, as may be seen by a reference to the Parliamentary Papers, disposed to waive this very important condition; but the Australians, with a good sense and a cor-rect appreciation of the merits of the case, so

1889. modified the article in an Imperial direction,
that, subject to the consent of the Colonial
Governments, the limits were enlarged within
which the squadron might be employed—a
power which, I trust, may never be required,
but which it is obviously wise to possess in
regard to the manifold contingencies of maritime war. I rejoice to make this acknow-
ledgment to the Australian public men who
negotiated this important agreement, and I
draw a favourable augury from it for future
conferences and consultations. But having
said this, I must also say as an impartial
judge and a lover of Australia, that the more
closely the agreement is examined the more
clearly it will appear that it is in a material
point of view an excellent bargain for the
Australian Colonies.

I have thus stated at some length the duties
which in the event of war would devolve upon
the British Navy ; let me ask—and the answer
can be given in much fewer words—what

proportion of this scheme of joint defence 1889.
ought to rest with the Colonies?

It is for them to place their great capitals,
overflowing with wealth and all the splendour
of a rising civilisation, in a position of adequate
defence, both for their own sake and to give
shelter to the Navy in time of difficulty. I
cannot pay too high a tribute to the energy and
patriotism of Victoria in the unstinted liberality
with which she has in time of peace prepared
for war—the surest way, in my opinion, of
averting war. The other Colonies have still
more or less to do before they can justly feel a
full sense of security; but I do not doubt from
what I have seen on the spot and from what
I know, that the public good sense of those
great communities will before long insist upon
the necessary amount of precaution being
taken. It is not really very much that is
needed, and when once the defences of the
large towns are complete, all that remains,
as I have already said, is to give some further

1889. organisation and unification to the local forces.
With this I believe that Australia may consider herself virtually safe from any serious
attack.

There remains the question of fortifying
King George's Sound in the south and Thursday Island in the north. It is a work which,
sooner or later, in the interests of Australia,
must be undertaken, and perhaps the sooner
the better; but I now only allude to it that
I may not seem to have overlooked it—and
though the suggestion may not be quite accept-
able to my Australian friends, I think that, all
things being fairly considered, the larger part
of the expense ought to be placed to their
account. Unless, indeed, the British fleet be
disabled or strangely out-manœuvred, I hardly
see how, with such precautions, a landing in
force on Australian soil would be possible.
The greater part of the enemy's naval forces
would probably be elsewhere, and though it is
never safe to repose upon calculations which

are optimistic or based upon the number of foreign ships of war that may at the present time happen to be in those seas, and though war, like everything else, is subject to the "unexpected," it is hard to suppose that with land works and land forces in fair order, and the Imperial squadron afloat, a descent of foreign troops would be practicable. The landing of 5,000 men means a very considerable fleet to carry the troops and to protect the transports, in which a certain proportion of cavalry and artillery must be conveyed.

Assuming, for the sake of argument, that we were at war with Russia or France, there are probably but two quarters from which attack would be possible—Vladivostock and the French Colonies. Of these, Vladivostock, if, indeed, not too far distant, can hardly be very formidable, while the railways connecting it with the interior are incomplete; whilst, as regards the French Colonies, they would, I think, have quite as much as they could do to hold their own. The danger, indeed, against which we have mainly to guard is not, I believe, as in former times, a loss of territory; it is rather some grave injury to our commerce—that commerce which we have won by such hard sacrifices, and which has made us —our life-blood, our vital breath; that which unites our Colonies to us—which has created and maintains our Empire—and without which England would become an over-crowded, pauperised, discontented island in the North Sea.

In thus speaking, I hope I need not say that I look with feelings of the utmost repugnance upon war with any of our neighbours. We hope that our relations with each member of the European family are as friendly as they can be; we believe that there is no real reason why our interests and theirs should be at variance; we covet no part of their possessions. But in arguing on such a subject as that on which I am speaking, we must for the sake of that argument assume that circumstances might arise which might drag us against our will into hostilities with some of those with whom we earnestly desire to be at peace. Nor need I say that not a word which I have spoken is intended to discourage action, or to lessen that patriotic and prudent spirit in Australia, which desires to take every reasonable precaution. My meaning is rather this— that when we in England and our kinsfolk on the other side of the Pacific have, in our several proportions, completed the work of defence, we shall have as strong a position as any country in these uncertain times can expect to possess; and, our house being thus set in order, we may, with an easy conscience, leave the issue to the great Disposer of human fortunes, without Whom neither ships, nor armaments, nor battalions are of avail.

I cannot draw these remarks to a conclusion without calling your attention to a matter which indirectly, but largely, concerns the questions of which I have spoken. A few

1889. weeks ago many of us were discussing Imperial Federation. We discussed it in an assembly composed of all shades of political opinion, and I rejoice that it was so. I will not allow that this great subject, which deals with the vital interests of the Empire, should belong to any one party in the State, and I should consider it unpatriotic on either side so to treat it. We have abundant questions to divide us, on which there must be factitious or factious difference of opinion, without importing our party variances into this one. But whilst we are discussing Imperial Federation at home, in Australia a considerable step towards it has been made by the action taken with regard to Inter-Colonial Federation; and I have always said and believed that this last would greatly facilitate, if it must not precede, the somewhat closer relationship which is involved in the former. Inter-Colonial Federation affects Australian interests primarily and directly; but even as regards the particular questions of defence to which I have referred, it is easy to 1889. see how greatly many of them would be simplified if we were dealing with a single Federal Government instead of many administrations and parliaments. In so large and complicated an arrangement as the Union of the Australian Colonies, there are very great difficulties— many of them imperfectly apprehended here in England, but not the less real or formidable. It was my privilege many years since, when I held the seals of the Colonial Office, to preside over the confederation of the disunited provinces of the Dominion of Canada; and I then learnt this lesson—that in such a work of imperial magnitude, where there were so many interests to conciliate, so many difficulties to overcome, great delays were inevitable, and great patience was necessary. The Confederation of Canada was the result of repeated conferences, consultations, concessions — in short, all the "give and take" which is the essence of English politics. My

1889. predecessor at the Colonial Office, Mr. Card-
well, a statesman whose memory is still justly
honoured, had with patience and ability paved
the way towards the great end in view, and
when I succeeded to his post, I received from
him every assistance. But confederation itself
was not possible till all preliminary measures
were complete, and above all, till public
opinion was ripe for the change.

Is public feeling ripe in Australia? That
is a question for Australians to answer, and one
on which any prudent Englishman will speak
with diffidence. I will not here attempt to
pronounce on it; but I may certainly say this
much—that whereas at a time which I perfectly remember there was in Australia little
or no feeling in favour of Inter-Colonial Federation, there are now many who desire it. The
appreciation of it has evidently grown. And
further, I will add, that the difference as to the
form of procedure which separates, or I may
now more correctly say, which separated, the

Prime Ministers of New South Wales and 1889.
Victoria a few weeks ago, appears to me, in
argument at least, to be narrow. It will be
in the recollection of many here present that
some years ago a Federal Council, which was
intended to provide a means of dealing with
matters of common interest to the Colonies,
was created. Unfortunately that Council did
not command universal consent ; to it Victoria
and most of the other Colonies of the Conti-
nent gave their adhesion; from it New South
Wales and New Zealand stood aloof. And a
preliminary divergence between the two leading Colonies as regards Inter-Colonial Federation has now grown out of the question
whether the Federal Council of Australasia
provides or can be made to provide efficient
machinery for united action as regards military
defence; or whether an entirely new departure must be taken in order to constitute an
Australian union with full powers of administration and taxation. Holding this latter

1889. opinion, Sir Henry Parkes, the Premier of
New South Wales, proposed that each Colony
should elect six members who should sit in
convention to frame a constitution for the
whole, Mr. Gillies, the Premier of Victoria, on
the other hand proposing that the representa-
tives of the several Colonies in the Federal
Council should meet Sir Henry Parkes and his
colleagues from New South Wales for the same
purpose.   The difference between these two
proposals was certainly a narrow one ; we have
heard that it has, in fact, been already sur-
mounted by a reasonable compromise, and I
cannot resist the expression of an earnest hope
that looking at this question, as I am sure Australian statesmen do, from an unselfish and
patriotic point of view, and merging private
and local ambitions in the interest of a common
Australia, they may achieve in a closer and a
more effective union an object of high policy
and value.   Australia has long been "fortune's
favourite," and has known few of the trials and

Subscribers wishing to purchase **Early Second Hand** copies of this work are requested to send their names to the Librarian, who will forward particulars of price as soon as the book can be spared for sale. ———————————

tempestuous troubles through which other 1889.
nations have passed; and a great constitutional
change, such as that of which I speak, proceeds
rather from the desire to grow in greatness and
prosperity than to escape from known dangers
and anxieties. But whatever the cause, we at
home can heartily wish her God-speed in her
desires, believing that in the growth of our
youngest child we see fresh guarantees for the
expansion of the Empire and the extension of
the British race.

IMPERIAL FORTRESSES.

HALIFAX.

BERMUDA.

GIBRALTAR.

MALTA.

IMPERIAL COALING STATIONS.

ESQUIMALT.

JAMAICA.

ST. LUCIA.

SIERRA LEONE.

ST. HELENA.

CAPE TOWN.

SIMON'S BAY.

ST. LOUIS, MAURITIUS.

ADEN.

COLOMBO.

TRINCOMALEE.

HONG KONG.

SINGAPORE.

THURSDAY ISLAND,

    TORRES STRAITS.

OTHER DEFENDED PORTS.

PORT OF SPAIN, TRINIDAD.

GEORGE TOWN, BRITISH

    GUIANA.

ASCENSION.

DURBAN.

KARACHI.

BOMBAY.

MADRAS.

CALCUTTA.

RANGOON.

PERTH.

ALBANY.

ADELAIDE.

MELBOURNE.

HOBART.

SYDNEY.

BRISBANE.

TOWNSVILLE.

AUCKLAND.

WELLINGTON.

CHRISTCHURCH.

LYTTLETON.

DEFENDED COALING STATIONS OF FOREIGN POWERS.

(Exclusive of European Waters.)

DIEGO SUAREZ (FRENCH).

REUNION (FRENCH).

SAIGON (FRENCH).

MARTINIQUE (FRENCH).

NEW CALEDONIA

    (FRENCH).

DAKAR (FRENCH).

VLADIVOSTOCK

    (RUSSIAN).

INDEX.

I.D.

N

THE END.

BRADBURY, AGNEW, & CO. LD., LONDON AND TONBRIDGE.